PRAISE FOR *ACROSS 7TH STREET*

"AN INCREDIBLE READ. RACHEL AND VINCENT'S LOVE STORY WILL INSPIRE YOU.YOU'LL LAUGH, CRY AND THINK."

- East Coast Book Review

"A MOVING AND POWERFUL STORY, FULL OF INSIGHT, WARMTH AND HONESTY."

- Scott Reviews

"HONEST, REAL, MOVING, EMOTIONAL, OFTEN HUMOROUS, *ACROSS 7TH STREET* IS A WONDERFUL BOOK."

- Coast Star News

"VINCENT AND RACHEL COME FROM DIFFERENT WORLDS, BUT THEIR STRUGGLES AND TRIUMPHS WILL INSPIRE YOU."

- Curtis Book Reviews

"A COMPELLING, EMOTIONAL AND BEAUTIFUL STORY. I COULDN'T PUT IT DOWN.....A TRIUMPHANT!"

- Oakdale Post

ACROSS 7TH STREET

ACROSS 7TH STREET

A Novel

By Marino Amoruso

Mymar Entertainment Press

 For information address MyMar Entertainment, 3300 Veterans Highway, Suite 103E, Bohemia, New York, 11716

ISBN: 978-0-9836931-1-6

Book design by: Café Urban

10 9 8 7 6

To Myra
For everything.....

ACROSS 7TH STREET

To Johanna
Thank you for
having me
All my Best

9/20/2012

OCTOBER 16TH, 1969

First off, let me say that this is not a baseball story. The reason I'm telling you this is that people who know me know I'm a baseball fanatic, so they'd just figure if I had a story to tell it would be about baseball. It's not. Not by a long shot it isn't. You see, not too long ago I saw a highlight film about the 1969 World Series on one of those all-sports cable TV networks. Seeing the film reminded me of what was the absolute happiest and best time of my life, but also the most devastatingly sad part of my life as well. Of course, none of it took place in 1969. It actually happened between September of 1962 and October of 1963. I know that doesn't make a whole lot of sense to you, but if you just keep listening I'm sure you'll understand. Anyway, I was at the final game of the 1969 World Series, so let's begin there.

I may have been the only fan in the ballpark that wasn't on his feet screaming on the day of October 16th, 1969. I was at Shea Stadium watching the New York Mets play the Baltimore Orioles in the fifth game of the World Series. The Mets led the best-of-seven series three games to one. It was the ninth inning and they were ahead by a score of 5 to 3 with two outs.

I had my little girl with me, who was three-years-old. We were about to witness the heretofore-lowly

New York Mets become World Champions.

The Mets came into being as a new team in 1962, four years after the Dodgers left Brooklyn, and for the first seven years of their existence they were absolutely horrible - one of the worst teams in baseball history. But all that changed in 1969. In what became known as the "Miracle of '69" the underdog Mets brought the entire nation to its feet, cheering, with their championship run.

The last out of the game came when the Mets left fielder, Cleon Jones, caught a fly ball to end the World Series.

The Mets were World Champions.

The miracle had come to pass.

The place went crazy. I have never heard such loud cheering in my life. It was as if seven long years of frustration and losing was let out in one enormous display of emotion. Total strangers were hugging each other. Some people were crying. Others stood staring out at the field in stunned disbelief, as if the miracle couldn't possibly have happened at all. Many thousands of people jumped on to the field as the Mets players ran for the safety of the dugout and clubhouse.

My beautiful little girl was asleep on my lap. I knew when I took her to the game that day that, at three-years-old, she would have little idea of what the hell was going on. It was her first baseball game. Still, her eyes widened in amazement when we walked into a ballpark packed with over 50,000 screaming fans. She smiled and pointed at everything. She made it through the first five innings before drifting off to sleep on my lap. I still don't know how she slept through all that noise.

I looked around in awe at the phenomenal spectacle unfolding before my eyes. It was so loud that I couldn't even hear the joyous screams of the people right next to me. I thought the deafening noise might wake up or scare my daughter. I looked down to see if she were still sleeping. She wasn't. But she wasn't upset or scared either. Instead, she stared up at me with those beautiful dark brown eyes. She had a bright smile on her face. At that moment all the emotion of the night hit me like a hammer to the back of the head. I felt tears well up in my eyes. I didn't want to start crying because I thought it might upset her. But somehow it seemed as if she understood what I was feeling.

Certainly I was ecstatic about the Mets winning the World Series, and I was happy because someday, when my daughter was grown, she could say she was there when the Mets won their first championship. But that wasn't the reason why my heart was full and my eyes were wet.

Instead, my mind drifted back seven years to a chilly September night in 1962 at the old Polo Grounds. The Mets played their first two seasons at the Polo Grounds before Shea Stadium was built. On that night I sat with a beautiful, dark-haired, brown-eyed girl who changed my life forever.

Her name was Rachel.

CHAPTER ONE

My father was a stone mason with a limp. The men who worked for him used to call him "Hoppy" behind his back. His left leg was normal but his right leg was twisted outward and his right foot pointed almost directly to the side. This was the result of a bullet he took in the thigh on Omaha Beach during the invasion of Normandy. He never talked about his experiences in the war. It always seemed like he just wanted to forget about all the violence and bloodshed he had seen and get back to a normal life. When we saw him around the house in his underwear we could see the hole in his thigh, and when we asked him about it, he just grunted, as if to say it was nothing. It was, however, something. The bullet had completely shattered his thighbone and the surgeons had to try and piece it back together. I'm sure they did the best they could under the circumstances, but my old man's leg somehow got twisted all around in the process. Often, when the weather got cold or damp, the leg would cause him great pain. I remember my mother rubbing it down with alcohol and wrapping hot towels around his scarred thigh. He never complained. He just bore the pain silently. That was his way.

My father's name was Angelo Anunnziato. His father, my grandfather Vincenzo, came to America from Bisceglie, Italy in 1909. Bisceglie is a fishing and farming village located at the top of the heel of the Italian boot on the east coast. Vincenzo came from a fishing family, but when he got to America the only work he could find was in construction. He soon found out that he was a wizard with bricks, stones, concrete and marble. An artist really. He started his own construction company specializing in stone and brick work and became quite successful. He moved from Manhattan to Sheepshead Bay, Brooklyn in 1919 and built a small brick house on Coney Island Avenue.

Grandpa Vincenzo died of a heart attack in 1938 just a few days after my father's eighteenth birthday. My old man took over the business. He had the same talents his father had. It was a good business. Brooklyn has literally thousands of brick and stone walkways and front stoops, not to mention houses and apartment buildings. There was always plenty of work.

My father married my mother, Felicia Gallo, in January of 1940. He was twenty and she was nineteen. They had known each other their whole lives. She grew up five doors down from him on Coney Island Avenue. They moved into the small brick house my grandfather had built, and my father's mother, Grandma Teresa, lived with us until she died in 1953.

I was born in March of 1941. In December of that year the Japanese bombed Pearl Harbor, and in August of 1942 my father was drafted into the army. He fought as an infantryman in Sicily and Italy and attained the rank of corporal. He was quite valuable to his commanding officers in these campaigns because he spoke fluent Italian. He won the Silver Star for bravery in combat in Italy.

On June 6th, 1944, my father was among the first wave of troops to hit the beaches at Normandy. He barely made it off the landing craft when a German bullet got him in the thigh. He was operated on and recovered in a hospital in London, and returned home in the fall of 1945. That's when I first got to know my old man. After all, he went to war when I was only a year old, and came back when I was four. My mother constantly talked about him when he was away and showed me pictures, but when he got back he was basically a stranger to me.

My old man was a quiet guy. He was either five-foot-nine or five-foot-eight depending upon which leg he was standing on. He had a thick chest and muscular arms from lifting and carrying bricks and stones since he was a kid. He had dark curly brown hair and dark olive skin. People always told me I got my skin tone and hair color from my old man's side of the family, but got my height and facial features from my mother's side.

My father worked hard, took care of his family, and was usually exhausted when he got home from work. He was a rabid Brooklyn Dodger fan and I became one as well. Even my kid sister, Maria, who was born in 1947, became a huge Dodger fan. The only time I saw the old man get really excited was when we were listening to a game on the radio or at Ebbets Field watching the Dodgers play.

Even though my father was usually bone-tired

when he got home from work, he always played catch with me on the sidewalk in front of our house. I would wait for him on the front stoop with the baseball gloves. He'd get out of his car and put his keys in his pocket, then I'd toss him his glove - he was a lefty - and we'd throw the ball back and forth for about an hour until my mother called us in for dinner. He never said much when we played, he just instructed me on the proper mechanics of throwing the ball or fielding a grounder.

As I got older I became more and more curious about my father's war experiences, but I could never get any information out of him. No matter what I asked him, I always got the same answer: "The army was okay," he'd say, "but the food really stunk."In 1950, when I was nine, we got a visit from the widow of one of my old man's army buddies. Her name was Myra Goldberg and her husband had been killed on Omaha Beach during the Normandy invasion. Turns out my old man and her husband, Isaac Goldberg, were best friends in the army - just two guys from Brooklyn who hit it off in basic training and looked out for each other in one battle after another.

My mother and father sat in the den with Mrs. Goldberg that evening, and mom served coffee and Italian pastries. I was sitting at the kitchen table doing my math homework. The kitchen was right next to the den so I could hear them talking as I worked. The story my old man told that night was the only war experience he had that I ever learned about in detail.

"It took me a long time to come over here," Mrs.

Goldberg said, "but I knew someday I would, because I need to know how Isaac died. I want to be able to tell our children."

I could hear my father kind of grunt a little when she said this, as if he also knew that this day was inevitable. If you knew my old man it was easy to tell that this was not something he wanted to talk about.

"I know from the letters that Isaac wrote to me that you and he were best friends and he thought the world of you," Mrs. Goldberg said.

"Isaac saved my life more times than I can tell you," my father replied.

"Call me Myra, please, and I know you saved his life, too, many times"

"But I couldn't at Normandy," my father answered, and as he said this, I could hear his voice tremble. I had never before heard so much emotion in my old man's voice. I put down my pencil, forgot about my math homework and listened intently.

"Please Angelo, tell me what happened the day he died. I could never get any information out of the army."

"They wouldn't know the details about anything."

"But maybe you do. Were you with him when he died?"

There was a long moment of silence. My father flipped open his Zippo lighter and lit a Lucky Strike cigarette. He chained smoke them.

"I was with him when he died," he said quietly, exhaling smoke.

"Did he suffer?"

"No Myra, he never even knew what hit him."

There was another long moment of silence. Mrs. Goldberg was waiting for my father to continue. So was I.

"We ran off the landing craft," my father said softly. "The beach was a nightmare. The Germans were just raking the beach with machine guns, rifle fire and shells. As soon as we got through the surf and hit dry sand, we dove for the ground. As I went down I felt a burning sensation in my right leg and I knew I was hit. I was bleeding pretty bad. Isaac must have heard me scream because he looked over at me and yelled 'You're hit in the leg, Dago!' That's what he called me, Dago."

My father paused and took another drag on his cigarette. "There was no way a medic could get to me, the gunfire was just too much. Next thing I know, Isaac rolls me over on my back, then takes the strap off his rifle and ties a tourniquet above the wound to try and stop the bleeding. He took a handkerchief out of his pack and wipes the blood and sand off the wound. Then Isaac reaches into his pack, takes out a packet of sulfur and puts it on the wound. I kept telling him I was fine and to keep his head down, but he wasn't listening to me."

My father stopped talking for a moment, and when he spoke again there was anger in his voice.

"I kept telling him to keep his God-damn head down, but he just wouldn't listen."

"Please go on, Angelo," Mrs. Goldberg said.

"Then he got up on his knees and starts searching

around in his pack for something to wrap the wound with. He found an extra shirt, so he rips that up and wraps it around my leg. He tied it real tight, like a tourniquet, to slow the bleeding. I kept saying, 'Isaac, what the hell are you doing? I'm fine. Keep your fuckin' head down!' Then my father cleared his throat. "Sorry about that, Myra, I didn't mean to use that word."

"Its okay, Angelo."

"So he says to me, 'You wanna bleed to death? Just shut the hell up and let me finish, you dumb-ass dago.' We were screaming at each other because the gunfire was so loud. You know, Isaac could be a real stubborn son of a bitch when he got his mind set on something."

"You don't have to tell me that," Mrs. Goldberg said.

"I guess not," dad answered, and took another drag on his smoke.

I got up from my chair in the kitchen and peeked through the doorway into the den. My mother was sitting next to my father on the couch, and Mrs. Goldberg sat opposite them on what was usually my father's chair. She was staring intently at my old man, waiting for him to continue. My father smoked his cigarette and stared at the floor. The smoke from his cigarette curled around his face. He just didn't want to go on, but he had no choice. He owed it to his friend and his friend's widow.

"That's the last thing he ever said to me, calling me a dumb-ass dago," my father said. "After he finished wrapping my leg, he looked up at my face to see if I was okay. That was it."

"How did it happen?" Mrs. Goldberg asked.

"Isaac looked at me, smiled, and then his head just fell on my chest." He took another long drag on his Lucky Strike. "The bullet went into the side of his helmet. He never felt a thing." My father looked up at Mrs. Goldberg. "I'm so sorry," he said.

Mrs. Goldberg dabbed at her eyes with a tissue. My mother rubbed my father's back. Mrs. Goldberg stood up and so did my dad. They hugged each other. When they sat down my father again said that he was sorry.

"For what?" Mrs. Goldberg said.

"Because if it wasn't for me, maybe Isaac would still be alive."

"Angelo, don't be ridiculous. You would have done the same for him. My Isaac always told our children that you put the people you love ahead of yourself. He loved you, and he died helping his friend. I am so proud of him, and his children will be, too. You have nothing to be sorry for. He was a hero."

"Everybody on the beach that day was a hero," my old man said.

"Angelo, I know how hard it was for you to tell me what you did. I appreciate it. I needed to know, and so do my children."

My mother walked Mrs. Goldberg to the front door when she left that evening. Mom told her that she was always welcome in our home, and to bring her children over for Sunday dinner some time. My father sat on the couch smoking. I stared at him. His eyes were wet. I had never before seen my father cry, and I never would again. He wasn't sobbing, but a few tears rolled down his cheeks, and I watched him wipe them away with his rough, callused hands.

My mother sat down next to him after Mrs. Goldberg left and again rubbed his back. My father lit another Lucky Strike from the first one. He looked over at my mom.

"There was one thing I didn't tell her," he said.

"What, Angelo?"

"Isaac was looking right at me when he got hit. When his head fell on my chest, he was still staring at me. I couldn't move and I couldn't move him. We just laid there like that for about two hours before the medics got to us. He just stared at me all that time with his dead eyes. My uniform was soaked with his blood. I couldn't tell his wife that. I just couldn't. When the medics finally got to us, they put me on a stretcher, and they just dragged Isaac away, like he was a dead animal or something. But I guess there were so many bodies on the beach that day that they didn't have much choice."

My mother hugged my father. He ground out his cigarette in the ashtray, got up and wiped the tears from his face with the back of his hand. I quickly ran back to my seat at the kitchen table. I suddenly realized that I was crying, too. I wiped my eyes with a dishtowel and made believe that I was working on my math homework. My mother came into the kitchen and put the uneaten pastries in the refrigerator. My father walked into the kitchen behind her. I jumped up from my chair and hugged him tightly. He was taken aback by my hug. It was not something I would normally do. I loved my father, and respected him, and I kissed him everyday when he came home from work and every night before I went to bed, but just throwing my arms around him for no apparent reason was a surprise to him. I was surprised at myself, but I had no control over my actions.

I let go of my dad then ran through the den and up the stairs to my bedroom. I lay down on my bed, staring at pictures of my Brooklyn Dodger heroes on the walls.

A minute later I heard my father slowly climbing the steps. Because of his limp, my father had a distinctive gait when he climbed stairs, and his knees always cracked. He walked into my room and sat on the bed.

"How much did you hear?" he asked.

"Everything."

He took a deep breath. "You know better than to listen to adult conversations."

"I know, dad, but I couldn't help myself."

He didn't know what to say. What could he say? He put his hand on my head, then leaned over and kissed my forehead.

"Dad, where was your friend Isaac from?" I asked.

"Only few blocks from here, on Ocean Parkway."

"He was a Jewish guy?"

"Yeah, why do you ask?"

"Well, all the Jewish people live over there in that neighborhood."

"So?"

"So, the nuns at school said that the Jews killed Jesus, and that they're all going to go to hell when they die."

"The nuns told you that shit, uh, stuff?"

"Yeah."

"Vincent, nobody knows for sure who goes to heaven or hell. It doesn't matter what religion you are. If you're a good person you go to heaven, and if not, you go to the other place."

"So your friend Isaac must be in heaven."

"I'm sure he is." He stood up. "Come on, let's go outside and have a catch.

"It's dark out, dad."

"Come on, the street lights are on. We can see just fine."

We played catch for two hours on the sidewalk in front of our house. It was the longest catch we ever had. We never said a word to each other. We just listened to the rhythmic smack of the ball hitting our mitts as we threw it back and forth. When we walked back into the house that night, my father put his arm around my shoulder. He had never done that before, and he never did it again.

My neighborhood was made up of mostly Italian families. For about four blocks on either side of our house, and for about three blocks behind us and in front of us, the area was pretty much a small "Little Italy." It was a great place to grow up. Everybody on our block was friendly, and in the spring, summer and fall, when people had their windows open, the aroma of Italian food cooking would make your mouth water. The houses in the neighborhood were small and built very close together. Some were made of brick and some made of wood. We all had tiny front lawns, maybe ten feet by ten feet at most. As kids we played in the street, on the sidewalk and in the school yard. We played stickball, punchball, handball, touch football, stoopball and a myriad of other games we made up using a pink Spaldeen rubber ball.

For about the first five years of my life I thought that everybody in the world had a last name that ended in a vowel. To tell you the truth, it wasn't until I started school, at St. Joseph's Catholic Elementary School, that I met a lot of kids who weren't Italian.

Just about every kid in my neighborhood had a nickname. The reason for this was that there were so many kids named Vincent, Anthony, Louis, Michael, Joseph, Ralph and other common first names for Italian kids, that if we didn't have nicknames for most of them, nobody would know exactly which kid you were talking about. I was known as "Vinny Bricks" because my old man was a stone mason. Vincent Palladino was called "Vinny Boots" because of his feet. As a kid his feet pointed straight out to the side, like a penguin's. He had to wear corrective boots for the first five years or so of his life to get his feet to point in the right direction. Hence, he became "Boots." There was "Vinny Black" who was of Sicilian descent and had very dark skin. I could go on and on, but you get the idea. My favorite nickname in the neighborhood belonged to Eddie Casola, who we called "Eyeballs." Eddie wore extremely thick glasses, which he himself called his "eyeballs." Without them he could hardly see at all.

My best friend growing up was Anthony "Mole" Martinelli. He was born a week after I was and our mothers were good friends. Anthony was born with a big mole on his chin. However, when we were about six, we went into his bathroom and, using a scissors, I cut it off as he had requested. There was blood everywhere and his mother had to rush him to the hospital to get stitched up.

Mole was the best athlete in the neighborhood and eventually signed a contract with the New York Yankees as a catcher, but he never made it to the big leagues.

Coney Island Avenue runs parallel to numbered streets in Sheepshead Bay, Brooklyn, and if you walked west on any of the cross streets near my house - Avenues Q, R, S, T, etc. - and you cross Seventh Street you were in the Jewish neighborhood, which was about twice the size of the Italian neighborhood. For me as a kid, going into that neighborhood was like visiting a foreign country. It was just so different from anything I was used to. First off, you never saw kids in the street playing any kind of sport. I just couldn't understand that. Some of the people dressed funny, too, especially the Hasidic Jews. I thought they looked really strange.

The men wore dark suits and large black hats –they looked like cowboy hats with large flat brims. They all had scraggily beards and had long strands of curled hair on the sides of their heads where their sideburns should have been. The women always wore long dresses or skirts and wore kerchiefs or hats on their heads. I would hear them speaking Yiddish to each other, which sounded to me like they were constantly clearing their throats.

The Hasidic Jews are a sect of Orthodox Judaism and were a small minority in the neighborhood, as it was made up mostly of "Modern" Orthodox Jews. Whereas the Hasidim are staunchly religious and devout, the Modern Orthodox Jews are not quite so strict and rigid in their behavior, beliefs and appearance, nonetheless they too are very, very religious.

The center of the Jewish neighborhood is on Ocean Parkway between Avenues Q and Z. Ocean Parkway isn't a big highway, like it sounds. It's a long boulevard that runs north and south from the amusement park at Coney Island in the south to Prospect Park in the north. There are two lanes of traffic going north and two lanes going south. On each side of Ocean Parkway there are esplanades that run the entire length of the parkway. The best way to describe the esplanades is to say they are very, very wide sidewalks - at least twenty feet wide. They are lined with big trees, there is grass on either side of the concrete sidewalk, there is a bicycle path, and wooden benches about every twenty feet or so.

Next to the esplanades on either side of the parkway there are service roads for the residents, and the houses and apartment buildings on Ocean Parkway line these service roads. These houses were huge compared to the ones we lived in. Some are three and even four stories high and most are sturdy brick structures. All the houses have large front lawns and concrete or brick walkways that run from the front door to the service road.

I rarely went into the Jewish neighborhood. When I did, it was for two reasons only. First, the esplanades were great places to ride your bike. On Saturday mornings all the Jews went to temple, so the esplanades were relatively empty. You could ride your bike at top speed from one end of Ocean Parkway to the other in the shade of the trees. It was impossible to do that in our neighborhood because of the traffic in the streets and the people on the sidewalks. At about twelve o'clock on Saturdays the temples let out and the Jewish people would come out to the esplanades to stroll and talk to their neighbors. That's when I left.

One thing I just couldn't understand was the fact that I never saw any of the Jewish kids playing any kind of sport on their big front lawns. If we had lawns that big in our neighborhood we would have been out there everyday having a catch or playing some kind of game, even tackle football. I thought it was a monumental waste of lawn space not to utilize them for sports.

The only other time my friends and I ever went into the Jewish neighborhood was for something I am not so proud of, but have to reveal anyway.

We went there to take money from the Jewish kids.

The thing of it was, the Jewish kids just wouldn't fight no matter what you did to them. A lot of the Jewish kids went to these Yeshiva schools and had to be in class about a half an hour before we did.

So we would stroll over to Ocean Parkway, stop a group of kids, and tell them that if they didn't give us their lunch money we would beat the shit out of them. They just handed over the money like it was a toll. I suspect that after the first few times we did it, their parents gave them double the money they needed for lunch. This way they could pay the "toll" we charged and still eat. The truth is, after a while we became pretty friendly with the kids we were extorting money from.

Every morning we would say hello to each other, then they would hand over their money and continue on to school.

My father was always in the Jewish neighborhood because it provided him with a lot of work. He was regularly doing jobs there, fixing walkways or stoops, or adding a small extension to a house.

I was working with my father in the fall of 1962 when I met Rachel Levy.

Mr. Levy wanted his entire walkway replaced and a new front stoop put in. He also wanted a brick wall built along his front lawn that bordered the sidewalk in front of his house. It was a big job. My father figured it would take us at least two weeks, maybe more. Mr. Levy had seen the beautiful work my old man had done on other houses in the neighborhood and hired him. We started the Levy job in early September of

1962.

In the following year I would experience the greatest love of my life, and also the most devastating heartbreak.

I was twenty-one in the fall of 1962 and had been working full time with my father for three years, from the time I had graduated high school. There was never any talk of me going to college, which is what I wanted to do. In those days, in most Italian families, the oldest son just went into his father's business. My father's brother, Uncle Peter, had a trucking company and his son, my cousin Bobby, drove a truck. My mother's brother, Uncle Nick, had a grocery store and his son, Mario, took over the store when Uncle Nick died. It was just the way things were in that generation. We weren't very big on education. In fact, no one in my family had ever been to college, let alone graduated. All the men either had their own successful businesses or fairly good jobs, but none had ever gone past high school, and some never even finished high school.

I felt differently about it. I wanted to go to college. Of course, my biggest dream was to play first base for the Brooklyn Dodgers, but the Dodgers left Brooklyn for Los Angeles in 1958, and by that time I had come to the realization that, although I was a good ballplayer, I did not have major league talent. My other dream was to become a journalist and photographer.

I had always loved to write, ever since I was a kid, and I loved taking pictures. From the time I got my first Brownie camera I was snapping away at everything, and I was good. I had a real eye for composition, framing and lighting.

I knew that in order to pursue a career as a photojournalist at a newspaper or magazine I had to get at least an Associate's Degree from a two year college.

My father just assumed that I would follow him into the construction and masonry business. I had worked with him every summer since I was thirteen and got pretty good at it. I had definitely inherited the skills he and my grandfather had in working with brick and stone, but it was not something I enjoyed. I finally spoke to my father about it when I was a senior in high school. I think he took it pretty well and we made a deal. I would work with him for three or four years and he would put part of my weekly salary directly into a bank account for my tuition.

My old man was sometimes difficult to work with. He was such a perfectionist that he would drive me crazy. It seemed like nothing I ever did was quite good enough. He always had to tinker with whatever job I was working on. Sometimes I just wanted to walk away because I got so pissed at him. I knew in my heart my father was just trying to teach me to do the job right, but it was still aggravating to be criticized all the time. He always used to say, "Vincent, I don't expect perfection, but I expect you to strive for perfection no matter what you do in this life."

I always worked hard and did the best job I could, but after three years of working with my father all I could think about was starting college.

I figured I'd work until the end of the following August - one more year - and start the fall semester in September at Borough Community College in Brooklyn.

The third day on the Levy job, a Wednesday, was the first time I saw Rachel. It was about three in the afternoon and I was by the front stoop stacking some bricks when I glanced up and saw her coming up the walkway to the front door. She wore a black skirt that went to just below her knees. She had on a white sweater over a red shirt, and she wore a kerchief on her head. I could see her long black hair hanging to her shoulders under the kerchief. In her arms she held schoolbooks. The notebook she held in front had a Borough Community College logo on it.

CHAPTER TWO

As Rachel got closer to me I noticed that she was petite, only about five-foot-three. But what struck me was her face. She was just beautiful. Despite the kerchief on her head and the plain clothes she wore, there was something about her that drew me in. The only way I can describe her is to say she looked exotic. She had beautiful, big brown eyes and a heart-shaped face. She actually reminded me of the beautiful actress, Audrey Hepburn, whom I had always had a "thing" for.

As she came toward me my mind raced trying to figure out something to say to her. When she got within a few feet of me I blurted out, "You go to college?"

She stopped in front of me. I was at least ten inches taller than she was.

"Excuse me?" she said.

"I said, you go to college, don't you?"

"Yes, I do."

For one of the few times in my life, I was at a complete loss for words.

"Why?" I asked.

"Why what?"

"I mean, what do you take in college?"

"Accounting."

"Oh, accounting. I thought about that."

"About what?"

"About taking accounting in college," I said, which, of course, was a total lie.

"Are you in school?" she asked

"Ah, no, not yet. I'm gonna start next year."

"That's very nice."

"Yeah, I'm a little late."

"For what?"

"I mean, a little late starting college. I've been working for my father for two years."

We stood in silence for a moment. I was trying to think of something to say.

"You take the city bus to school everyday?" I asked

"Yes, I don't like riding the trains."

"Me neither, it's too hot in the summer, and it always smells like, ah, it always smells bad in the trains."

I was going to say that the trains smell like stale piss, which they do, but I caught myself before I blurted that out and made a complete ass of myself.

"The trains do smell," she said. "Sometimes they smell like a dirty bathroom."

Yes! She thought they smelled like stale piss, too. But of course she wasn't going to say it in the crude way I would have said it.

"I'm gonna go to Borough Community College, too," I said. "I need to get over there and pick up a course book so I can see what I'm gonna take."

"I think I have one inside. You can borrow it if you'd like."

"That would be great, thanks."

Suddenly we heard a voice from the front door and we both turned toward it at the same time.

"Rachel!" her father said. "Come in the house, now!"

Mr. Levy stood in the doorway. When I saw him my immediate thought was that now I knew why Rachel was small. Mr. Levy was only about five-foot-six, and very skinny. He wore dark pants with a white shirt and a black tie. He had a fairly long beard and wore a yarmulke on his head. He looked to be in his late fifties.

I turned back toward Rachel, "My name is Vincent," I said.

"I'm Rachel," she answered. Then she smiled and quickly turned and walked towards the front door.

I didn't follow her with my eyes because I thought her old man would be watching me and I didn't want to give him the wrong idea.

I looked toward Ocean Parkway and watched the cars speed by for a few moments. It's hard to describe, but I felt a bit light-headed. I had never felt like that before after talking to a girl for just a few moments. I thought to myself that maybe this girl had just knocked me off my feet, or, maybe because I skipped lunch that day I was getting a bit woozy from not eating. It had to be one or the other. I was hoping it was the former and not the latter. I decided to eat my lunch. It was a little after three o'clock.

"Hey pop!" I yelled to my old man, who was working at the other end of the walkway, "I'm gonna eat my lunch."

"Don't take forever," he said. "We have a lot to do today."

I took the meatball hero my mother had made for me and went and sat on a bench on the esplanade in front of the Levy house. I ate the sandwich in four bites. I was starving. But even after I finished, I still felt a bit light-headed.

It must have been meeting Rachel that was making me feel that way. Or, maybe I was coming down with something. I had no clue. All I knew was that I actually felt pretty good.

The rest of the workday flew by. Late in the afternoon I heard the front door open and I hoped it was Rachel coming out the door. When I looked up I saw Mrs. Levy coming down the walkway. I knew it had to be her because she looked like an older version of Rachel. Mrs. Levy was also petite, with the same long, dark hair and big beautiful eyes. She nodded and smiled as she walked by me and, although it was over eighty degrees that day, I noticed she wore a long sleeve shirt. She looked to be a few years younger than her husband.

I spent most of the day hoping that Rachel would come outside and we could continue our conversation. She never did. I also hoped she had maybe peeked out a window to watch me working. I figured she would be impressed by my strength as I lifted bricks and stones. Then I thought that this was a really stupid thing to think. Why would she look out the window to see some sweaty guy lifting bricks? I went over our short conversation in my head many times that afternoon as I worked. I came to the conclusion that I was basically a total idiot who must have sounded like a complete ass.

Vincent.

Rachel had never actually met anyone with that name. She knew a lot of Davids, Sauls, Irvings and Mannys, but not a Vincent. She was sitting at the kitchen table doing an assignment for one of her classes, but all she could do was think about Vincent. She was in her second year of a two-year accounting program at Borough Community College, and when she graduated in June, she would be the first woman in the Levy family to receive a college degree, even if it was only an Associate's Degree.

Mr. Levy walked into the kitchen and sat down next to her.

"You were talking to that boy outside this afternoon?" he said.

She looked up at him. "Yes."

"About what?"

She put down her pencil. "Nothing really."

"It must have been something. You were talking."

"I'm not allowed to talk to somebody?"

"I didn't say that. I just wanted to know what you were talking about."

"He asked me about college."

"Why?"

"I don't know. He was interested in what I was

taking."

"Why would he want to know that?"

"Because he said he was going to college next year."

"That, I doubt."

"What are you talking about?"

"Look Rachel," her father said, leaning forward, "Italian people really don't believe in education like we do. Mostly they are laborers, like that boy. He will work hard and make a good living, but he will never be an educated man."

"Why are you telling me this?"

"You are an adult now, and these are things you should know."

"What? That Italians aren't educated people? I'm sure there are many educated Italian people."

"That too I doubt. I am almost sixty-years-old and know more of the world than you do. I have rarely come across an educated Italian in all of my experience."

"Dad, you're a diamond wholesaler in the diamond district in Manhattan. All the people around you and in your business are Jewish. Everybody in this neighborhood is Jewish. Where would you come across an Italian person, other than the ones you hire to work on the house?"

"Believe me young lady, I know. Besides, we all know that many of them are connected to organized crime."

Rachel couldn't believe what she was hearing. She loved and respected her father greatly, but some of his opinions were just so old fashioned.

"Dad, in my school there are students of all different nationalities, including Italians. And besides, it's wrong to say that all of them are gangsters. That's like saying all Jews are cheap."

"Perhaps, but I have not heard of many famous gangsters who weren't Italian."

Rachel shook her head. "Well, what about gangsters like Bugsy Siegel and Meyer Lanksy and Dutch Schultz? They were all Jewish. I learned about them in a class I took on the history of New York City."

"They are not our kind of Jewish people."

"Dad, why are we having this conversation? All he did was ask me about college. It's not like I'm going to run off and marry him."

"You will never run off and marry anybody. You will finish school, then take a trip to Israel, and then you will come to work for me. You know I have always had the need for somebody I could completely trust to take care of our books and financial records. And then, if the right Jewish young man comes along, it will be time to marry."

"Dad, listen to me." She put her hand on his arm. "I can't even think that far ahead. I have a year of school to go and I have a lot of very hard courses this year. I need to concentrate on school for now. Just this week I have three big tests to take."

Mr. Levy got up from the table. "Finish your homework, Rachel. We have no need to talk about this any further. The young man will be here for the next two weeks until the job is done. Perhaps you should not encourage him by talking to him."

"I'm not encouraging anybody, dad."

Rachel couldn't tell her father what she was really thinking. She had been thinking about Vincent since she came into the house. He was so different than the boys she knew in the neighborhood. First off, he was tall. He was over six-foot tall, with olive skin and dark curly brown hair. He wore a tank top tee shirt and had wide shoulders and very muscular arms. He also seemed very sweet, polite and shy. She smiled when she thought about him awkwardly trying to make conversation with her. She knew, of course, that to even think of him in this way was strictly forbidden. She couldn't even imagine what her family's reaction would be if she ever dated a non-Jewish boy, let alone an Italian boy who was a manual laborer.

Then again, Vincent did say he was going to go to college. It was all fantasy anyway. She knew her future was somewhat pre-determined. Like her father said, she would finish school, go to Israel and work on a kibbutz for three weeks, go to work for her father when she returned, and then marry a nice Jewish boy - probably from the neighborhood.

The problem was all the young Jewish men she met did nothing for her. She had dated a few boys from the neighborhood and just never felt anything for any of them. She felt no excitement, no thrill.

She had no desire to see any of them again – at least not in a "date situation." They were all the same. They were polite and respectful, but boring, and they were not very handsome or even very manly in her opinion.

She picked up her pencil and tried to get back to

work. But she kept thinking about Vincent. She had spoken to him for maybe a minute, yet she couldn't get him off her mind. She had never felt anything like that before. She had actually peeked through her bedroom window late in the afternoon to watch him work. He was a very strong young man. She couldn't believe how many bricks he could pick up at one time. He did it so easily. And when he picked up the bricks the muscles bulged in his arms. She thought of some of the boys she had dated in the past few years. She couldn't even conceive of any of them picking up a pile of heavy bricks. She could just see their arms shaking as they tried. It made her smile.

Mrs. Levy into the kitchen and saw Rachel smiling.

"You certainly look happy young lady," she said.

"Why shouldn't I be happy?"

"Of course you should be. That's what your father and I want most for all our children, for you to be happy. And what is making you happy today?"

Rachel knew there was no way she could tell her mother that she was thinking of the handsome Italian boy who was working on their house.

"I'm just in a good mood today," she said.

"Good for you. Now finish up your homework. We'll be eating dinner in an hour or so."

Mrs. Levy walked out of the kitchen and Rachel tried to get back to work. It was fun and exciting to fantasize about Vincent, but she knew that's all it could ever be, a fantasy.

I ate dinner really quickly that night. I was meeting my friend Mole to play some handball at the schoolyard. My mother made macaroni with white clam sauce, which I just about inhaled. Then I asked to be excused and was out the door.

Mole was slapping a pink Spaldeen ball off the brick wall of the school building when I arrived.

"Hey Bricks," he said. "Ready to get your ass kicked?"

Mole had just finished his third season in the New York Yankee farm system. He was a catcher and a good one. We often discussed how Yogi Berra was getting old, and by the time Mole was ready to make the big club, their other catcher, Elston Howard, would be getting older as well. Mole could just step right in and become the Yankee backstop.

"Sure you can kick my ass," I said. "You've been taking naps all day. I been out there lugging bricks around."

"I don't want to hear excuses."

"No excuses. Let's just sit for a minute before we start. I just ate two bowls of macaroni and clam sauce."

We sat with our backs against the wall of the school.

"Where you working?" Mole asked.

"Over on Ocean Parkway. Doing a stoop, a walkway and a brick fence. It's a big job"

"Over there with the chosen people, han?"

"Hey, we get a lot of work over there."

"So listen," he said. "I saw Rosemarie today."

"Oh yeah, what'd she have to say?"

"Nothing much. She was asking how you were

doing. You know, she still has a thing for you."

Rosemarie Carbona was a girl I dated for a year after high school. She was a beautiful girl, but not too bright. We had lost our virginity to each other in the backseat of her father's car on a summer night in the parking lot of a shopping center on Flatbush Avenue. After that all she ever talked about was getting married. I couldn't even think about that. I knew I had to work for my old man, and then I wanted to go to college. She even offered to work and put me through college. The problem was, I really hadn't loved her all that much. In fact, I wasn't sure I ever loved her at all. She was a pretty girl and we got along okay, but I just didn't feel any excitement or magic when I was with her.

"I know Rosemarie still has a thing for me," I said to Mole. "It's just that I don't have a thing for her."

"I know, besides, have you ever seen her mother?"

"Yeah, what does that have to do with it?"

"Everything, man, everything. I have this theory that if you want to know what a girl is going to look like in twenty or thirty years, check out the mother. Rosemarie's mother has got to be at least 300 pounds and still gaining."

I smiled, "Yeah, she is a rather large woman. But that don't mean Rosemarie's gonna be fat."

"Well, it ain't always the case, but it is a lot of the time. I don't know if I would want to take that chance. Let's face it, if a woman the size of Rosemarie's old lady rolled over on you in bed, they'd need a spatula to scrape you off the sheets."

"Now Mole, is that a nice thing to say?"

"Just speaking the truth my friend. Just speaking the truth."

I needed to talk to somebody about Rachel. I just couldn't get her off my mind. I wasn't sure if I should bring her up to Mole. Then I figured, what the hell? We had been best friends since we were babies. If I couldn't say something to him, then who?

"I saw a real good looking girl at the job today."

"Really?" he said. "Where?"

"On the job, on Ocean Parkway."

"On the street?"

"No, at the house we're working at."

"A Jewish girl?"

"Yeah, a Jewish girl."

"Bricks, you better run as fast as your dago legs will carry you. You don't want to be involved with one of them."

"What the are you talking about?"

"You ever see how Jewish women boss around their husbands? It's like the men got no balls at all. Hell, you remember how when we were kids we used to take the lunch money from the Jew boys over on Ocean Parkway? If anybody ever tried to steal our lunch money, we would have kicked their ass."

"Since when are you an expert on this stuff?"

"Just take my word for it. Besides, if you ever came home with a Jew, your mother would have a fit. Your old lady is the most Catholic person I know. She'd be running to church everyday, praying that your Jewish girlfriend got run over by a bus or something."

"Whoa, let's not get carried away here. I just said I saw a pretty girl. That's all. All of a sudden you got me dating her and my mother going crazy."

"Just trying to nip it in the bud."

"Yeah, right, Mole Martinelli, expert on romance."

"I know a little. You gotta understand, girls really like ballplayers. When we come out of the locker room after a game, there's dozens of 'em waiting for us."

"So because you got baseball groupies in Shitwad, Arkansas, or wherever it is you play, that makes you an expert on Jewish girls from Brooklyn?"

"You got a point there."

"I know, but I gotta tell you something, this girl Rachel kind of looks like Audrey Hepburn."

"The movie star?"

"No, the cafeteria lady at our high school, you asshole, of course the movie star."

"How do you know her name?"

"I talked to her when she came home from school."

"She's still in high school?"

"No, college. She goes to Borough Community, where I'm going next year."

"Seems like you got a plan cooking in your head."

"No, nothing like that. Just telling you the facts."

"Well, you better get one fact straight. I don't care how beautiful this girl is, the whole idea of Vinny 'Bricks' Anunnziato, full-blooded wop, dating a Jew from Ocean Parkway is probably not a good idea."

The sad part was that my friend Mole was probably right.

CHAPTER THREE

I couldn't wait to go to work the next day. By the time my father finished his breakfast I was outside waiting by the truck.

"You looking forward to work today or something?" my father said.

"No, just got up a little early."

"You stayed up late watching the Mets game, I figured you'd be sleeping in."

"The Mets lost again. Meanwhile, the Dodgers keep winning. Why the hell did they ever leave Brooklyn?"

"You and about four million other people wonder about that."

As we drove over to Ocean Parkway I was hoping that we'd get to the Levy house early enough so I would see Rachel coming out the door to catch the bus for school. Then again, maybe she didn't have school today and she'd be around all day. It was eight in the morning.

We drove up to the Levy house and I saw Rachel walking down the esplanade to the bus stop at the corner of Ocean Parkway and Avenue W. She carried her books, but today she wasn't wearing a kerchief. She stopped at the corner to wait for the bus.

A plan hatched in my head.

If she walked along the esplanade to and from the

bus stop, then I would take my lunch break at about three o'clock. That was the time she had gotten home from school the day before. I thought that maybe I could eat my lunch on a bench by the bus stop and when she got off the bus, I could walk with her for a couple of blocks to her house.

Why was I thinking this stuff?

I had never thought of anything like that before. Who was I kidding? Mole was right. My being interested in a Jewish girl was just stupid. Our lives and backgrounds were so different in so many ways. Besides, why would she be interested in me? Her family obviously had a few bucks, and I was just some dago manual laborer working on their huge house. She probably thought I was one rung higher than the family pet on the evolutionary chain. On top of that, she was so attractive, she probably had a boyfriend already. Her boyfriend was probably some kid I had taken lunch money from way back when.

I tried to reason with myself and be logical and sensible about the whole thing, but it didn't work. All I could concentrate on was my plan to be on a bench on the esplanade when Rachel got home from school. I was just hoping that she got home at the same time every day.

I worked like a machine that day. I figured it would make the time go by more quickly. It didn't. Every time I looked at my watch it seemed as if only five minutes had passed. Then something struck me. Rachel was a college girl. I thought she'd be very impressed if, when she walked by me sitting on the bench eating my lunch, I was reading a book.

Problem was, I didn't have a book with me. I thought of a solution for this, too. When I took my mid-morning break, I would run home and get my copy of *To Kill a Mockingbird.* It was my favorite book. I had read it in eighth grade, and had read it at least six times since then. My house was only eight blocks away. If I ran both ways, I could do the round trip in about twenty minutes. I had no idea how I was going to explain it to my old man, but I knew I'd think of something.

At eleven o'clock I told my father that I was going to take my break. I also told him that my stomach wasn't feeling so good and I wanted to run home and take some Alka- Seltzer.

"Must have been the clam sauce last night," he said.

"Maybe, I just don't feel that hot."

He tossed me the keys to his pickup truck. "Take the truck," he said.

My old man was a God.

I got back to our house, ran upstairs to get the book, then went into the bathroom and flushed the toilet. I knew when I got downstairs my mom would ask me what I was doing home, so, by flushing the toilet, I could tell her my stomach was a bit off and ask her for some Alka-Seltzer. Was I a genius, or what?

I was back at the job site in less than twenty minutes. I went right back to work. My father was looking at me as if I had two heads.

"What the hell is with you today?" he said. "You get up early, you're working like a maniac, you don't feel good but you're still going a mile-a-minute."

"I'm fine, dad. Just doing my job."

"Okay, whatever you say."

At about five minutes to three I told my father I wanted to take my lunch break. He had eaten at about noon, but I had told him that my stomach still didn't feel right so I could put off eating my sandwich until about three o'clock.

"You feeling better now?" he asked.

"Yeah, I think I'm getting hungry."

"Okay, take about twenty minutes."

I would take longer if I had to. I mean, what was he going to do, fire me? I ran to the truck and grabbed my lunch bag. I stuffed the paperback copy of *To Kill a Mockingbird* into the bag, and then walked down the esplanade to the bus stop on the corner. I didn't want to sit on a bench too close to the bus stop, as that would have been too obvious. I picked one about forty feet from the corner.

I ate my sandwich in three gulps. I didn't want to have a mouthful of salami and cheese when Rachel came by, so I wiped my teeth with my napkin to make sure there weren't any stray pieces of food stuck there. Then I settled back and opened my book to the middle. It didn't matter. I had read the book so many times that I knew exactly where I was in the story.

Every time I heard a bus coming up the street I looked to see if it was the bus that stopped on Rachel's corner. Finally, at about ten after three, a bus stopped. The first person off was Rachel. I got that light-headed feeling again when I saw her. I looked down at my book, but kept peeking to my right to see how close she was getting. There was a slight breeze and her hair was blowing. My God, she looked so beautiful. I really had no idea how I was gong to pull this off. Should I notice her, or should I let her notice me? What if she didn't notice me and just walked right by? What if I stopped her and she thought I was being too familiar or too forward? And most importantly, why was I acting like a complete ass by setting up this whole ruse just to have the opportunity to talk to this girl. It suddenly dawned on me how ridiculous the whole thing seemed. Then again, I was sure people have done stranger things for love.

Wait a minute.

Love?

Where did that word come from?

What the hell was I thinking?

"Hello," I heard.

I looked up and Rachel was standing in front of me.

"Hey Rachel, how you doing?"

"Hi Vincent. You know, I never actually met anyone named Vincent."

"Actually my real name is Vincenzo, after my grandfather, but Vincent is the American version, but everybody calls me Vinny, except my close friends who call me Bricks."

I was babbling like an idiot.

"Your friends call you Bricks?"

"Well, there's a lot of guys named Vincent in my neighborhood, so because my old man is a mason they call me Bricks so we all know the difference between me and all the other Vincents. Does that sound dumb?"

"No, not at all. So what should I call you?" she asked.

"Vincent is fine."

"What are reading, Vincent?"

"Oh, *To Kill a Mockingbird*. It's my favorite book. I like to read when I'm on my lunch break."

This was the first time I had ever read anything on my lunch break, other than the sports section of the *New York Daily News*.

"That's a wonderful book," she said.

"The book is great, and so is the movie."

"I never saw the movie," she said.

"You never saw *To Kill a Mockingbird*?"

"No, we don't go to the movies much."

"It just came out this year."

"Well, I didn't see it."

"Did you ever see the movie *Sabrina*?"

"Yeah, I think I saw that once on *Million Dollar Movie* on Channel 9. Why do you ask?"

"Well, it's just that you kinda look like the star of the movie."

Rachel blushed. She actually blushed and then smiled. When she did, it felt as if a jolt of electricity shot through my body.

"You really do," I said. "You kinda look like Audrey Hepburn."

"You think I look like Audrey Hepburn? I think maybe you need glasses."

"No, my eyesight is just fine."

"Thank you Vincent, that was very sweet of you to say."

"Nobody ever told you that before?"

"No, no one ever did."

"Well, it's true. You do look like her."

She stood looking into my eyes, smiling. At that moment it seemed as if the world was spinning. I wanted to tell her how beautiful she looked. I wanted her to sit next to me so I could be closer to her. Then again, I had been working hauling bricks all day in the hot weather and I probably didn't smell very good.

"How long do you think you'll be working at my house?" she asked.

"My dad figures probably two weeks, give or take a few days."

"How do you lift all those bricks at the same time?"

"Excuse me."

"I said, how do you lift all those bricks at the same time? I saw you out my window yesterday and you were carrying a big stack of bricks."

So she did look out the window while I was working. Maybe I wasn't as crazy as I thought.

"I've been carrying bricks around since I was about thirteen. That's when I started working for my father, you know, during the summer when school was out."

She looked at her watch. "I better get home. My father is going to wonder where I am."

She hesitated, then suddenly sat down next to me. I felt another rush of electricity race through my body. She looked at me and her face was only a few inches from mine. I was hoping I didn't smell too bad.

"Listen, Vincent, my father didn't like it so much that we talked yesterday."

"Why?"

"It's kind of hard to explain. It's just that he's very strict and very Jewish, and he thought I might be flirting with you, and being you're a goy, that got him upset."

"A what?"

"A goy."

"I don't know what that is, I'm Italian."

She smiled. "I know, a goy means someone who's not Jewish."

"We were just talking about college."

"He doesn't care what we were talking about." She looked up at the sky, then back at me, like she was trying to find the right words. "See, my father kind of has everything planned for me. I finish school, I take a trip to Israel, I go to work for him as a bookkeeper, then I meet a nice Jewish boy, get married, and have a bunch of kids. I don't know why, but he has this crazy fear that I'm going to run off with some goy and ruin it all. But that could never happen."

"Israel? You're gonna go to Israel?"

"Well, I'll be going over there to work on a kibbutz for three weeks. All my cousins have done it."

"What's a kibbutz?"

"Well, it's this kind of big farm that many families live and work on. Kind of like a big community farm. They grow most of their own food and raise livestock, and they sell what they don't use." She paused, looked down at the ground, then at me again. "Look Vincent, please don't try and talk to me when we're around my house. My father just won't like it."

"I can't believe that. He seems like a nice guy."

"He is, he's a wonderful man. It's just that he's got his ways. If he sees me talking to you he's going to question me every time."

"Then why can't we talk here on this bench? He can't see us from your house. It's two blocks away."

"I know, but maybe someone from the neighborhood will see us and tell him. That would be even worse."

"Then where can we talk?"

Rachel looked into my eyes, and then looked down. "I don't know if we really can," she said.

It was as if someone had punched me dead on in the stomach.

"You can't be serious," I said.

She looked up at me and I knew she was.

"I'm sorry Vincent."

"That's just not right," I said.

She got up from the bench. I looked up at her. She looked at me sadly, then turned and started to walk down the esplanade. I had to say something. The whole thing just seemed so absurd.

When she was about fifteen feet away from me, I stood up and said, "Well you do look like Audrey Hepburn, and Audrey Hepburn is absolutely beautiful."

She stopped for a moment. I could tell that she wanted to turn around and look at me. But she just kept walking. I sat back down on the bench. I picked up my book and flung it out into the street. What the hell was I thinking? I should have known better.

I went back to work and right away my old man could tell the difference in my mood. Whereas all morning I had been working at a fast pace and seemed happy to be alive, now I was moving in slow motion.

"What the hell happened to you?" he asked. "You look like somebody just shot your dog."

"Nothing dad. I just feel like shit again. My stomach is bothering me." And this time it really was. To that point in my life I had never had such an empty feeling in my stomach. Talk about having the rug pulled out from under you.

When we got in the truck to go home that night, my father handed me a brown paper bag that was on the seat.

"Before you got back from your lunch break the Levy girl went into her house and brought this out to me," he said. "She asked if I would give it to you. She said it was a course book or something from Borough Community College."

I grabbed the bag from him, took the book out and stared at it. I opened it to the first page and saw that Rachel had written a note to me on the title page of the book.

Vincent,
If you want to keep talking, then we can meet at a bench on the esplanade on the corner of Ocean Parkway and Avenue Z on Monday. That's far enough away so that my father will never see us. I can get off the bus there after school and we can talk for a short

while. I know you're only going to be working at our house for about two weeks, so at least we can enjoy each other's company for a couple of weeks.

Rachel

My stomach suddenly felt better again.

"Awright," I said to myself.

"What's that?" my father asked.

"Oh, nothing, just looking at some courses to take. Let's get home, I'm starving"

"I thought your stomach was on the blink."

"Yeah, it was, but I feel a helluva lot better now."

Rachel had had serious second thoughts about writing the note to Vincent in the Borough College course book. In the end she convinced herself that there was no harm in it. After all, he would be gone in a couple of weeks and why not enjoy his company for a few minutes each day during that time?

She told him that they shouldn't speak anymore, but in her heart she didn't really mean it. He was interesting, funny, smart and handsome. When she was with him she felt an excitement inside her that she had never felt before. She found herself thinking about him all the time. She only hoped that he wasn't mad about what she had said to him on the esplanade about not ever talking to her again. Maybe he was so angry with her that he didn't want to have anything to do with her. She would understand if he felt that way. He had every right to feel that way. If he wanted to meet with her it would be great, but ultimately nothing could come of it anyway. They'd spend some time together then go on with their separate lives. Still, she had never felt in her heart what she felt when she saw him and heard his voice. It was a kind of magic she had never experienced before. And it all happened so quickly. She made up her mind to take it day by day.

On Saturday morning I was supposed to meet my friends Mole Martinelli and Eyeballs Casola at Stramiello's Café, which was a small sandwich and pastry shop about a block from my house. We were going to have some coffee and pastry then head to the schoolyard to play some basketball. When I met them at the café, I told them I had to run over to the house my father and I were working at on Ocean Parkway. They kept asking me why we had to go there, but I just ignored them until we got to Ocean Parkway.

"Tell me again, why are we standing here on Ocean Parkway?" my friend Mole asked when we arrived in front of Rachel's house.

"Yeah," Eyeballs chimed in, "exactly what the hell are we doing here?"

Mole, Eyeballs and I were standing on the esplanade in front of Rachel's house, which was close to the corner of Avenue U and Ocean Parkway.

Mole stood there with his hands on his hips. He was six-foot-three, about 180 pounds and built like the athlete he was. He had light brown hair and dark eyes. The girls loved him. Eyeballs was almost as tall as Mole, but about thirty pounds lighter. He was as skinny as a rail. He had curly, jet black hair and, of course, wore those thick glasses with thick black frames. He was always pushing the glasses up on his nose. They must have weighed a pound. The three of us had been close friends our whole lives.

"Look, are you guys gonna help me here or what?" I said.

"Help you with what?" Eyeballs asked. "I'm still not sure why we're here, are you Mole?"

"I have no clue."

"Here's the deal," I said. "I gotta go from here to Avenue Z, then come back again, and see how long the whole trip takes. And we gotta do it now because all the people around here are in temple so no one will see us."

"Who the hell we hiding from?" said Mole.

"Look, that's where I'm working," I said and pointed to Rachel's house. "I don't want them to see me out here so that's why we're here now. They're in temple."

"Yeah," grumbled Eyeballs, "and I should be eating a cannoli with a cup of espresso."

"Okay Bricks, you want us to do this with you, you gotta tell us the exact reason why you gotta walk five blocks and back, and time the whole thing," Mole said.

I told them the reason. I wanted to make a dry run to Avenue Z and back to see exactly how long it would take me. I had thirty minutes for lunch, so if I was going to meet Rachel at the corner of Avenue Z and Ocean Parkway on Monday, I had to know exactly how long it was going to take me to get there and back, and then I would know how much time I had with Rachel. I explained all this to my friends.

"You can't be serious," said Mole. "This is that Jewish girl you were telling me about?"

"I'm as serious as a heart attack," I answered.

"What Jewish girl?" asked Eyeballs. "What are you guys talking about?"

"Here's the deal, Eyes," Mole explained. "Our boy Bricks here is, like, you know, falling in love with this Jewish girl who lives in that house." He pointed to Rachel's house. "Don't ask me why he's gotta walk five blocks to meet her."

"Whoa, wait a minute here," Eyeballs said to me. "I thought you and Rosemarie Carbona were kind of still going out."

"Where you been, Eyeballs?" Mole said. "Bricks and Rosemarie broke up, like, a year ago. Besides, Bricks decided that Rosemarie was gonna be a three hundred-pounder like her old lady."

"I never said that, Mole."

"Whatever. Now our pal's got this thing for this Jewish girl named Robin."

"Rachel," I corrected him. "And it's not this great love affair or anything. She's just really great to talk to, and she goes to college at Borough Community, and I'd rather spend my lunch break talking to a pretty girl than sitting on a stoop eating my sandwich."

"Bricks, who are you kidding? You're gonna walk ten blocks round trip cause she's great to talk to? There's more going on there than you're saying. Besides, why do you gotta go five blocks to meet her?

She only lives right there."

"Look, it's a long story," I said. "Just come along with me on this."

"Okay, whatta you wanna do?" asked Eyeballs. "Let's get this over with. I'm getting hungry."

"Well, we gotta walk the five blocks to Avenue Z, and we gotta walk fast, but we can't run. I don't wanna be running. If I run down the middle of Ocean Parkway in the middle of the day, someone's gonna think I mugged somebody or robbed a house or something, and the next thing you know I'm gonna be on the ground with handcuffs."

"Are you saying that the Jewish people in this neighborhood are a bit paranoid?" Mole asked sarcastically. Why would they call the cops if they saw some Italian kid running at top speed through the middle of their neighborhood? You're not being fair to our Jewish brothers and sisters."

"Are you gonna be a wise ass or are you gonna walk with me?" I said.

"Wait a minute here, Bricks," Eyeballs said as he cleaned his extraordinarily thick glasses. "Does your old lady know you're seeing a Jewish girl? Not for nothing, but didn't your mom want you to become a priest at one point? I mean, she can't be too happy about you dating a Jew."

"What the hell is this with all these questions?" I said. "I'm not dating her. She ain't my girlfriend."

"Yet," added Mole. "And if she does become your girlfriend, your mother is not gonna be too happy. She's the most Catholic person I know."

Mole was actually right to a certain extent. My mom was *very* Catholic. And as far as my father went, I wasn't sure how he would take it. He was always so quiet about things.

Then I thought to myself, why am I even thinking this way? I had only talked to Rachel twice in my life, and the last time we had spoken she basically told me to take a hike because of her old man. She then wrote me that note, which made my day. Now here I was timing my walk to and from our meeting place to get the maximum time with her. I could understand why my friends were confused about the whole thing. I wasn't that clear about it myself. I wasn't sure exactly why I was doing this.

The rational part of me knew that to start a relationship with an Orthodox Jewish girl wasn't a practical thing to do. But, for the first time in my life, I was listening to my heart and not my head.

"Let's just walk up to Avenue Z," I said. "All three of us time it. Just follow my pace."

We started walking at a pretty fast pace, but not running. Of course, the whole time my friends were making wise ass remarks about the Jewish girl and me. If being a wise ass were an Olympic sport, Mole and Eyeballs would tie for the gold medal.

It took about six and a half minutes each way, which meant a total of thirteen, so I would have about seventeen minutes to talk to Rachel. Once we got back to Avenue U in front of the Levy house, Mole started with the questions again.

"Now tell me again why you gotta walk five blocks

to meet her?" he asked.

"I didn't tell you the first time," I said

"Well tell us now," Eyeballs said.

"Look, her father isn't very happy about the fact that she is talking to a goy boy," I explained.

"A what?" they said together.

"A goy."

"What the hell is a goy?" asked Eyeballs.

"Sounds like a body part that gets infected," added Mole. "You know, like, my goy is all inflamed."

"It's a Jewish word for someone who ain't Jewish," I said.

"So you're gonna walk ten blocks so the old man don't see you?" Eyeballs said.

"Not for nothing, Bricks, but you're outta your mind."

"Come on, Eyes," said Mole in his wise ass way. "This is true love we got here. Italian boy loves Jewish girl, but Jewish dad don't like dago boy, so dago boy walks ten blocks to see his true love. It's all so romantic I think I'm gonna throw up."

"How you gonna throw up?" said Eyeballs. "We didn't eat nothing. We got nothing to throw up."

"You know Eyeballs, you got a point there," said Mole. "I think the goy boy here owes us a cannoli each from Stramiello's Café for helping him with his mission of true love."

"You guys are just asses," I said. "Mole, you don't gotta do nothing for five months until you report to spring training in Florida. And Eyeballs, you work in your old man's deli eating mozzarella all day and flirting with old ladies. I'm the only one here who actually works."

"Good," said Mole, "you got the most money, so let's head over to Stramiello's and you pay."

We went to the cafe, had a cannoli each with a cup of espresso and it tasted really good. I sat in the café wondering if Rachel had ever had a cannoli and a cup of espresso. I wondered if she even knew what they were.

On Monday morning I was again waiting by my father's truck. He came out of the house, saw me standing there and just shook his head. This was not my usual behavior in the morning. Sometimes I even fell asleep in the passenger seat when we drove to a job. Now I was just raring to go in the morning.

When we got to Rachel's house she had already left for school. I told my old man that I was going to start taking my lunch break at three o'clock most afternoons.

"Why?" he asked.

"Well, last Friday, when I ate that late, I kinda liked it. When I eat in the early afternoon I get kinda tired."

"Vincent, what's up with you?" he asked.

"Whatta you mean?"

"Vincent, I know you. You're not really acting like yourself these past few days."

How do I handle this one?

"I don't know dad. I think I'm just excited about starting school next year. I been waiting a long time."

"I know son. I appreciate that. I'm sure gonna miss you on the job."

"Why? You always find something wrong with whatever I do, other than lug bricks around."

"That's not true Vincent. You do great work. I just know you're capable of better work sometimes. Whether you're in school, or just sweeping the front stoop, don't ever do things half-assed. If you're gonna do something, do it one hundred percent, or don't do it at all."

I couldn't argue with my father. That's what he believed in and that's how he lived his life. He was no hypocrite.

CHAPTER FOUR

On Monday the time moved slower than it had on Friday. I worked like a maniac all day, hoping to make the time fly by. Every minute seemed like an hour. I did think about what Rachel and I would talk about. We would have exactly seventeen minutes together before I had to head back to her house. Actually, it would have been nice if we could have walked back together. Then again, somebody might see us as we got closer to her house and tell her old man and that definitely wouldn't be a good thing.

At one point in the early morning, while I was working on the Levy stoop, Mr. Levy came out the front door. I looked at him and smiled and said good morning, but he didn't even acknowledge my presence. He just glanced at me and kept walking. He usually left for his office in Manhattan about eight in the morning, and got home between two and three o'clock. When he walked by me I actually wanted to jump up, race after him and ask him why it was such a big deal to him that Rachel and I had talked. I wondered what went on in his head. Did he think I was any less of a person because I wasn't Jewish? I found myself starting to get mad at him.

What?

Does he think Jews are superior to Italians?

What an arrogant prick.

Of course, thinking of Rachel's father as an arrogant prick was not going to help the situation.

As I worked that morning I did come to one very important conclusion; that I was fooling myself. I had somehow convinced myself, from a rational and realistic standpoint, that I was meeting Rachel because she fascinated me and I enjoyed being with her. I also figured, what the hell, in another week or so we'd be through with the job and I'd probably never see her again. But that morning I finally understood that, although we had only spoken two times, I was falling for her. She just gave me a feeling inside that I had never experienced before. Ever. To deny what I was feeling was just plain stupid. Then, the rational side of me kicked in and I'd think, well, we'll just see what happens.

Finally, after what seemed like twenty-four hours, it got close to three o'clock. I told my old man I was going to take my lunch break, and also told him I was going to walk along the esplanade as I ate. He just grunted and I was on my way. I walked fast, shoved my sandwich down as I walked, and wiped my mouth and teeth with a clean napkin I had put in my pocket in the morning for that express purpose.

Rachel was sitting on the bench waiting for Vincent. She kept glancing to her left to see when he came into view. She kept telling herself that there was no point in even meeting him. She knew realistically that nothing could ever come of it. She also knew she was fooling herself. Whenever she saw Vincent she got a feeling inside of her that was exciting and new. She often pictured him in her mind - his smile, his dark skin, his muscular build - and when she did, it made her heart feel full like it never had before.

Despite being nineteen the truth was, she'd had very little experience with boys. She remembered the first time a boy kissed her. She was fourteen and it was at Daniel Weinstein's Bar Mitzvah. She was dancing with Howie Epstein to a slow song, and he just looked at her and then quickly kissed her on the mouth. She didn't get mad or upset, she was just a bit surprised. She also recalled that he tasted like creamed herring. She dated a few boys as a teenager, and in the past year had actually gone out with Howie Epstein two times, both times they went to dances at the temple social center. She couldn't imagine any person more boring than Howie. All he ever talked about was how he was going to take over his father's accounting firm when he got out of school, and what he was going to do with all the money he made. It seemed to Rachel that he was always trying to impress her, trying to make her think he was a "good catch" or something.

She knew that boys were attracted to her by the way they looked at her and always seemed to be trying to impress her. She was not impressed with anyone. All the "nice Jewish boys" she knew were just plain boring and unattractive. It was like they were all cut from the same mold.

For some reason Vincent made her think about

things differently. Just this morning she took much more time than usual picking out what she was going to wear.

She chose her blue skirt because it was a bit shorter and a little tighter than her other dresses. And she put on her pullover white shirt because it accented her figure better.

She told herself she chose these clothes not because she wanted to appear more attractive to Vincent, but because she just hadn't worn them in a long time and she looked good in them. She also knew she was fooling herself. She wanted Vincent to think she was beautiful. He had already told her that she looked like Audrey Hepburn. In the end, she rationalized that it would only be a week or so before he was gone, and it would be fun to be with him while it lasts. In her heart, however, she couldn't deny the magic and wonder she felt. She just hoped that he had actually found the note she wrote in the book and would meet her at the bench. What if he hadn't found the note? What if he hadn't even looked in the book because he was upset with her? Then, out of the corner of her eye she saw Vincent about a block away coming towards her. It felt like her heart was going to leap out of her chest.

I saw Rachel sitting on the bench. I started to walk faster. I didn't want to walk too fast and look like an overanxious idiot, but I wanted to get there as soon as I could to have more time with Rachel.

When I got about twenty feet away she looked up at

me and smiled. She stood up from the bench and I went to her.

Then it just happened.

We embraced each other for a short moment. She felt absolutely wonderful in my arms, so small and fragile.

Then we both jumped back, embarrassed.

"I'm sorry," I said. "I didn't mean to be so familiar."

"That's okay."

She sat down on the bench and I sat next to her.

"I have to be back to your house in about twenty-five minutes," I said, "unless my old man is gonna wonder where I went."

"I have to get back, too, otherwise my father is going to wonder where I am."

We were silent for a moment.

"Thanks for the note," I said.

"I was only hoping you'd see it."

"I saw it as soon as I opened the book."

"Were you looking at possible courses to take at school?"

"The truth?"

"The truth."

"No, I was kinda pissed off and just turning the pages out of frustration, I guess."

"At least you're honest. I guess I would have been upset, too. I really didn't mean to...."

"Forget it, Rachel," I interrupted. "It doesn't matter."

"It's just that my father can be so stubborn sometimes."

"Actually, my mother's a bit like that. Not so much my old man."

"It's the opposite with me. My mother seems more accepting of things than my father does. I think it's because she was in the camps and after seeing what she saw there, she became more open-minded about things."

I wasn't sure exactly what Rachel was referring to when she talked about the camps.

"The camps? You mean, like, your mother went to summer camps or something?"

As soon as I said this, I suddenly realized what Rachel meant; the concentration camps. I felt like a complete fool.

"I'm sorry," I said. "I see what you mean. I just didn't...."

She smiled. "It's okay Vincent."

"Does she ever talk about it?"

"No, never. But I know she lost most of her family. My mom's from Poland. She lost her parents and brother to the Nazis. She was lucky to survive. She was just a teenager then, I think maybe eighteen or nineteen at the time. After the war she came to Brooklyn because she had a distant cousin who lived here and they took her in. Sometimes I think she feels guilty about that."

"About what?"

"About surviving, I think, while the rest of her family died. That's why she always wears long sleeves, even in the summer, to hide the number on her arm."

I had no idea what Rachel was talking about.

"What number?" I asked.

"In the concentration camps the Nazis used to tattoo a blue number on everybody's arm to keep track of each prisoner."

"You know, when I saw your mother come out of the house the other day, I noticed that she was wearing a long sleeve shirt even though it was about eighty degrees outside."

"It's because of that number. I guess she thinks if people see it, they'll ask her about it, and it's just something she really doesn't want to talk about. When I was about thirteen she told me she was in a concentration camp and escaped, and that was it. We never really talked about it again. I've asked her about it quite a few times, but she never wants to talk about it"

"I'm sorry. God, that must have been awful for her. I don't know much about the concentration camps, just what I saw in books about World War II. My father told me once that I had a great uncle, my grandmother's brother, who died in one of the camps."

"Was he Jewish?"

"No, no, he was a soldier in the Italian army during the war. He got drafted into the Italian army and couldn't get out of Italy to come to America. Then the war started."

"I don't understand."

"Well, during World War II Italy and Germany were allies. That was because of the Italian dictator, Mussolini. The Italians really didn't want to fight the Americans, and most of them actually hated

Mussolini. Anyway, Italy officially surrendered to us in 1943. So after that, the Germans tried to send all the Italian soldiers that weren't captured by the Allies to the Russian front. A lot of the Italian soldiers refused to go, so they were sent to these labor camps and the Germans just worked them to death. My Uncle Franco, Grandma Teresa's brother, wouldn't go to Russia so they sent him to a camp called Dachau."

"Really? I was never told about anyone else who died in the camps, just the Jews."

"No, there were millions of others, at least that's what my father tells me. Our family didn't even know what had happened to Franco. He used to write letters to my grandmother in Brooklyn, then in 1944 the letters just stopped coming. And from then until 1952 nobody knew what had happened to him. Then my grandmother got a letter from the Italian government saying he was dead and buried in the Italian Soldiers War Memorial near Dachau. She cried for days. I think she always thought that Uncle Franco was going to come walking through the door someday. She always had hoped that her brother was alive, but we all knew he had to be dead. My grandmother died a year later"

"I'm sorry," she said softly.

"Is your father from the other side, too?" I asked

"No, he's a German Jew. His family came here years ago, in the late 1800s or something. He was born here. In fact, he was in the American army during the war."

"My father, too."

"But my father didn't do any fighting. He speaks fluent German, so they stationed him in London. He used to translate the intercepted German radio messages or something like that. He never really talks about it. What did your dad do?"

"My father was an infantryman. He fought in Sicily and Italy, then got wounded at Normandy. He got shot through the leg. That's why he limps. In fact, his best friend in the army was a Jewish guy from this neighborhood named Isaac Goldberg. Isaac died on the beach at Normandy. I heard about that when I was a little kid."

A look of stunned amazement came to Rachel's face when I told her this, like she couldn't believe what I was saying.

"What?" I said. "What is it?"

"That has to be my Uncle Isaac. Of course I never met him, but I know of him."

"Are you serious? You can't be serious?"

"My father's older sister, Aunt Myra, was married to him. She's been remarried for a while now, so we don't see her that much anymore."

"Well then, your aunt was at my house when I was a little kid. She came to see my dad because she knew from the letters Isaac wrote to her that he and my dad were best friends in the war. She wanted to know how her husband died. My father told her, and I was in the kitchen listening. That's how I know about it. My dad never talks about the war."

"I don't believe this, Vincent. I mean, it has to be my Uncle Isaac. How many Isaac Goldbergs can there be who died at Normandy and were married to a woman named Myra?"

"Well Rachel, this is Brooklyn you know."

She smiled, "You're right, there could be a few hundred."

"Yeah, but I know it's gotta be the same guy. I can't believe this. You're uncle saved my dad's life at Normandy."

"He what?'

"Saved my father's life."

I told her the story I had heard my father tell to Mrs. Goldberg all those years ago in our den. The story about the day Isaac died on Omaha Beach.

"Oh my God," she said after I finished the story. "I really can't believe this."

"This is really strange, it's like we had a connection all those years ago," I said. "Our families were connected. My father once told me, years later after I had heard the story about Isaac, that he and Isaac used to pass the time talking about the Brooklyn Dodgers. It kind of kept their minds off the war and the fact that they could get killed at any second."

"You know, my father used to really love the Dodgers. He was a big fan. I remember when I was a little girl he was always listening to games on the radio. Then the Dodgers left Brooklyn and went to California or something, and he lost all interest in it. I don't know much about baseball."

"Well, you know Rachel, baseball is life"

"Baseball is life?"

"Sure, think about it. Sometimes you win, sometimes you lose and sometimes it just rains. I loved the Dodgers when I was growing up. Now I root for the Mets, but they really stink. Hey, did you know that Jackie Robinson's wife's name is Rachel?"

"Well, I've heard of Jackie Robinson. I know he was the first Negro to play in the, you know, big baseball leagues. And I've heard my father say to his friends that Jackie Robinson was the most exciting player he ever saw. That's about it."

"See, you do know something about baseball. Now you know that Jackie's wife's name is Rachel."

She smiled and I swear my heart started to beat faster. There were cars zooming by on Ocean Parkway, horns blaring, busses stopping at the corner, but I was so focused on Rachel's face, I really didn't see or hear anything. It was an amazing feeling.

"Have you ever been to a baseball game?" I asked.

"No, I don't think I've ever actually seen a whole game. I see the kids playing little league in the park, or sometimes people in the neighborhood have the game playing on the radio. That's it."

"You haven't even seen a game on TV?"

"No, my father doesn't watch baseball, and neither do my two little brothers, so where would I see a game?"

"Whoa, that's hard to believe."

"It's true."

"Would you like to go?"

"Go where?"

"To a baseball game. We could go see the Mets at the Polo Grounds."

"Oh, I can't do that.

"Why not?"

"If my father ever found out I went to a game with you, I mean, just us talking on the bench here is kind of crazy. He'd be pretty upset. Plus, what would I tell him? Where would I say I was going?"

"We could think of something."

"I could never lie to my father."

"I wouldn't ask you to do that."

I knew in my heart Rachel wanted me to think of something, anything, so we could figure out how to go to a game together. Don't ask me how I knew. I just did.

"Well, how about this?" I said "I'll look at the schedule and see if there's an afternoon game coming up. Then you can go to school, but I can meet you somewhere and we can go to a game."

"I can't do that," she said. "It costs money to take my classes. It wouldn't be fair to my father."

"There's gotta be a way. We'd have fun."

"Well, sometimes, at night, I take the bus over to the Brooklyn Public Library to study" she said. "Maybe I could just get on the bus like I'm going to the library, and then meet you somewhere. Then I don't have to lie to my father. He'll just think I'm going to study like I do sometimes. But I'm always home by ten-thirty or eleven at the latest."

"That might work. The games start at seven, and if it's a quick game, you'd be home by, like say, maybe ten-thirty or so."

"I think that would be okay."

"I'll look at the schedule and let you know tomorrow."

My mind was racing. I couldn't believe what was happening. Rachel and me at a baseball game. Suddenly it dawned on me that maybe my seventeen minutes was up.

"Oh man, what time is it?" I said.

She looked at her watch. "Twenty five after three."

"I better get going. I'm already a minute and a half behind."

She looked a bit puzzled by my statement. "A minute and a half behind?"

"I hate to admit this," I said, "but on Saturday I walked down to this bench and back from your house to see how long it took. This way I knew how much time we had."

She smiled and I got that electric feeling through my body again.

"What's so funny?" I asked.

"You did that for me?"

"Yeah."

"That's so sweet, Vincent."

"I came in the morning cause I figured you guys would be in church, I mean temple, so you wouldn't see me. Man, I gotta go."

And then, just like that I leaned over and kissed her on the right cheek. I don't know why I did it. I just did because it felt like the natural thing to do. She looked at me for a moment, and then she kissed me on the cheek. I felt that wonderful electricity again when her lips touched my cheek.

I jumped up from the bench. "I'll see you when you get back to your house. And we'll meet here again tomorrow."

"Just don't say anything to me at my house. I'm sure my father will be watching."

"Don't worry, I won't. But you can give me a little look if you want to."

As I walked quickly down the esplanade it felt as if my feet weren't even touching the ground.

CHAPTER FIVE

Vincent arrived at Rachel's house a few minutes before she did, and was on his knees working on the walkway when Rachel got there. She glanced down at Vincent and smiled when she passed him as she walked to the front door. When she stepped into the house she could hear her parents talking in the kitchen.

"When did she call?" her mother said.

"Just a few minutes ago," answered her father.

"Was she sure it was Rachel?"

"Please Anna, Mrs. Rabinowitz has known Rachel since she was a baby. How could she mistake her for someone else?"

"And Mrs. Rabinowitz said she was kissing the boy? On a bench by Avenue Z?"

"That's what she said."

Rachel felt an emptiness in the pit of her stomach. Mrs. Rabinowitz had obviously seen Vincent and her on the bench. Why couldn't people just mind their own business? Why, of all people, did it have to be Mrs. Rabinowitz who saw them? She was the biggest gossip in the neighborhood. Before long everybody for five blocks around would know that she had kissed Vincent on the cheek.

Of course, by the time the story got around it would

become more than just a peck on the cheek. Who knows what people would hear and think?

She put her books down on the hallway table and walked into the kitchen to confront her parents. Both were standing by the table. As soon she walked in, her mother sat down but her father remained standing.

"Rachel," he said, "why do you deceive and defy me?"

She didn't answer him. She just walked to the table and sat next to her mother.

"Answer me young lady. Why do you deceive and defy me?" her father asked again.

"I'm not deceiving or defying anyone."

"But you are," said Mr. Levy. "Mrs. Rabinowitz called just a few minutes ago and told us that she saw you kissing a boy on a bench on the esplanade. She said it was a boy in a tee shirt and dungarees, so I'm sure it's that boy Vincent who's working here. I asked you not to talk to him, not to encourage him. Is that your idea of obeying me? To kiss him in a public place for all the world to see?"

"Dad, it was just a peck on the cheek. I was walking home from the bus stop and he was sitting on a bench eating his lunch. We talked for a while, and then I gave him a little kiss good-bye on the cheek. Is that so terrible? Is that so wrong?"

"First of all, why did you get off the bus at the Avenue Z stop instead of Avenue W like you usually do? And yes, it was wrong to meet this boy, especially when I expressly told you not to talk to him or encourage him. I never thought I would say this, but I am ashamed of your behavior, Rachel."

"That's not fair to say to her, Henry," said Mrs. Levy.

"And what, Anna? Now you are taking her side?"

"No Henry, I am not taking her side. But I think you are making more of this than it is. So what? She met a boy she likes to talk to and they became friendly. I'm sure our daughter understands that nothing can ever come of it more than a friendship. She knows what's expected of her."

Rachel was happy that her mother was defending her. But in one regard her mother was wrong. Something was definitely happening between her and Vincent. It was something she had never felt before, and it was wonderful and exciting. There was no way she could express this to her parents, although she did have a sense that perhaps her mother would understand her feelings. She knew in her heart that she was falling in love with Vincent. To try and deny it was foolhardy. And it didn't feel wrong. In fact, the complete opposite was true. She had never had a better feeling in her life.

"Mom, dad," she said, "I don't see anything wrong with talking to Vincent. I enjoy it very much. He's so different than the boys I have known around here."

"He is not one of us, Rachel," said her father. "I am sure he is interesting to you because he is different than what you have known. But that is no reason to kiss him in a public place and cause us embarrassment and shame."

"Please Henry," said her mother, "it is not that bad.

You make it sound like they were necking on a bench for the entire world to see. It was just a kiss on the cheek. Don't you believe your daughter?"

"That is not the point," he answered. "The point is that I told Rachel not to speak to or encourage the boy and she defied me."

"Henry, she is a grown woman now and entitled to make her own decisions. You must believe that we have raised her well and she will use good judgment."

"Anna, would you say that kissing a boy in public is good judgment?"

"Perhaps not, but it is not as bad as you are making it."

Rachel didn't know what to say to her parents. What they feared most was that she would fall in love with Vincent, and that was certainly happening. Yet, she couldn't tell them the truth.

"Dad," said Rachel, "I'm sure you don't know this, but one time many years ago Aunt Myra was at Vincent's house."

Her father looked at her oddly, not understanding what she meant. "Aunt Myra was where?" he asked.

Rachel told her parents the story of how Aunt Myra's husband, Uncle Isaac, had saved the life of Vincent's father on the beach at Normandy, and how Mr. Anunnziato and Uncle Isaac were like brothers during the war.

After she finished the story her parents stared at her in silence for a moment, not knowing what to think, or what the story had to do with the subject at hand.

"Rachel," her father said softly, "Uncle Isaac was

obviously a brave man who died for his country while saving the life of his friend, but that has nothing at all to do with what we are discussing now."

"But it does, dad. Uncle Isaac and Vincent's father came from different backgrounds, just as Vincent and I do, but in the end it didn't matter. They were just people."

"And there are differences among people," he replied. "To be in war is one thing. It has nothing at all to do with you encouraging that boy in Brooklyn in 1962. Don't you see the difference?"

"No, I don't dad."

"Well then, that is what parents are for. To teach you and steer you in the right direction when you are lost. You will understand when you have children."

"I am not lost, dad."

"Rachel," her mother said, "what do you feel for this boy?"

She couldn't tell them the truth, not yet.

"I just like him as a person," she said. "He is funny and smart. He is interesting. And dad, he's a big baseball fan. He told me today that he was a big Dodger fan just like you were, and that Rachel is also the name of Jackie Robinson's wife."

"That is all well and good," said Mr. Levy. "Still, you are forbidden to see this boy under any circumstances. Is that clear young lady?"

"Henry, isn't that a bit much?" said her mother.

"Anna, what if she continues to see this boy, and being young and foolish, she thinks she loves him? Do you not understand the problems this would cause?

She is too young to know this."

Her father spoke of her as if she wasn't even in the room at all, and Rachel found this insulting and demeaning. For the first time in her life she felt a defiance and anger at her father she had never experienced before.

"Henry, you are angry now," said Mrs. Levy. "Perhaps you should think a bit before you give orders to your daughter. I myself would not forbid her to talk to the boy because I would trust her judgment in not letting it go too far. She has always been a sensible and smart girl."

"Anna, I am still the head of this house, and Rachel still lives under my roof, and as long as she does, she will live by the rules I have set." He turned to Rachel. "Is that very clear to you young lady?"

"Dad," she said, "I have never before until this moment realized how close-minded you are sometimes. I wouldn't have believed it."

This was the single-most defiant thing she had ever said to her father, and after it came out she couldn't believe she said it.

"Rachel," said Mr. Levy, "someday you will understand."

Rachel looked at her father and shook her head. "I don't think I'll ever understand."

"Rachel, if you are interested in boys, why don't you see Howie Epstein?" Mr. Levy asked. "He's a good boy. He comes from a good family. He has always liked you. He'll inherit a good business. You've gone out with him before."

"Dad, Howie Epstein is an idiot," said Rachel.

Her mother laughed quietly.

"Something is funny here?' her father asked.

"Dad, Howie is a pompous jerk, and he smells bad, like he needs a shower."

Mrs. Levy could no longer suppress her laughter, and let out a rather loud giggle.

"What is so funny, Anna?"

"When Rachel is right, she is right," she said. "Howard Epstein is a pompous ass, and he has horrendous body odor."

"Okay, so forget Howie Epstein," her father said. "But you must also forget this Italian boy. Tomorrow I will have a little talk with this boy's father when he comes here to work. He, too, is a father and will understand my concerns. If he does not, then I will get another worker to finish the job he has started."

"Dad, you can't do that."

"When it comes to the welfare of my daughter, it is my right as a father to do what I think is best."

"To do what is best for you, or for me?" said Rachel.

"For you, Rachel."

"If you cared what was best for me, you wouldn't forbid me from talking to someone just because he is not Jewish, and you think I will fall madly in love with him and ruin all your plans. What are you afraid of?"

"I will tell you what I fear. I fear that my daughter will not act like a responsible adult, and will continue to deceive and defy me."

"Then you do what you have to do," said Rachel. "And so will I."

Rachel got up from the table and left the kitchen to go upstairs to her bedroom. She sat down on her bed and stared at the floor. She had never before spoken to her father in that tone of voice. She had never been so defiant. A part of her was ashamed by the way she behaved, but another part of her felt strong and, for the first time in her life, independent. It felt good. It was exciting. It almost felt the same as when she was with Vincent.

Rachel could actually understand why her father was the way he was. It was how he was raised. Her father's family came to America in the mid-1880s from Germany. They were not poor immigrants like many who came to America. In fact, the opposite was true. For hundreds of years in Germany her father's family had been prominent jewelers.

When her great grandfather, Moishe Levy came to America he was well financed by his family. He bought a big house in Brooklyn and rented offices on the West Side of Manhattan. After careful research into various aspects of the jewelry business in New York, Moishe Levy decided to become a wholesale jewelry dealer. Within a very short time the business prospered greatly. When he died he passed the business on to his only son, Jacob. Then, when Jacob died, the business was inherited by his only son, Rachel's father Henry, who had worked with Jacob from the time he was a little boy.

Henry Levy had led a privileged life from the day he was born. He went to private Yeshiva schools all through his childhood, and then graduated from

Manhattan College. His four years in college was really the first time that Henry Levy had any kind of exposure to people who were not Jewish. The only other length of time he had spent around non-Jews was when he was in the army during World War II and stationed in England as a translator. His exposure to the non-Jewish world did nothing to shake his faith or beliefs.

Henry Levy was not in any way spoiled by his affluent upbringing. His parents instilled in him a strong work ethic. They taught him about commitment and responsibility to his family and his faith. He learned to have respect for other people, regardless of their beliefs. He lived by a very simple philosophy - and Rachel had heard him say it many times - “Live and let live.”

Despite being in his late fifties, Henry Levy was somewhat naïve when it came to people of other ethnicities and religions. Having spent the majority of his life living and working with mostly Jews, he tended to believe the stereotypes he heard about people who came from different backgrounds than his. He was not a prejudiced man. He was just a man with very little life experience outside his own Jewish world.

Henry's parents had been very strict and observant Orthodox Jews and they passed this on to their son. His entire world was defined and shaped by his faith and the Jewish culture. The Brooklyn neighborhood where he had grown up and now lived in had always been a Jewish enclave. The wholesale jewelry business in New York was made up primarily of Jewish people. Everybody who worked for him was Jewish.

Rachel's father had never known what it was like to wonder where his next meal was coming from. He never had to look for a job to support his family. Even the Holocaust during the war had no direct effect on him. The Levy family in America had lost touch with the Levys in Germany many decades before the war started. Rachel was sure that members of her father's extended family in Germany died in the Holocaust, but her father had no knowledge of what members of his family might have perished in those dark times. This, of course, was the complete opposite of her mother who had experienced the horrors of the Holocaust as a young girl in Poland.

Henry Levy had a vast knowledge of the history of the Jewish people and all they had faced and overcome throughout the centuries. He was very proud of Jewish history, heritage and culture, and was overjoyed at the establishment of Israel as the Jewish homeland after the war. Rachel knew that was why he was so insistent that she spend some time there after she finished college. He believed it would give her an understanding of her rich heritage that she could not find in Brooklyn.

Rachel knew her father was a generous man with a warm heart who would do anything for his family. Still, he was so rigid and strict when it came to his religious beliefs. He wanted nothing more in this life than for his three children - Rachel and her two younger brothers - to carry on the Jewish traditions and religious beliefs he was raised with. That is why her feelings for Vincent scared her. Her father would not understand. She couldn't even imagine how he would react if he knew that she was falling in love with an Italian-Catholic boy.

She had tried to rationalize to herself that she would see Vincent for only a couple of weeks until he finished his work at her house, and there was nothing wrong with enjoying his companionship during that time. But she knew in her heart that she was falling in love with him.

She had never felt this before. It was wonderful and it was frightening. She convinced herself to take it a day at a time and see what happened. All she knew for sure was that, for the time being, her father could not know how she felt about Vincent, nor that she was seeing him.

We got to Rachel's house about eight o'clock on Tuesday morning. She had already left for school. I immediately went to work on the stoop, while my father concentrated on the walkway. About fifteen minutes after we began work, Mr. Levy came out the front door. He was obviously headed to his business in the city, which my father told me had something to do with wholesale jewelry.

He walked down the path, but stopped when he got to my father. I thought maybe they were talking about the job we were doing, but Mr. Levy was quite animated and kept pointing at me. My father glanced over at me a few times. I thought, this can't be good at all. I couldn't hear what they were saying and tried to look uninterested.

Mr. Levy finished telling my father whatever it was he had to say, and then left. My father stood with his hands on his hips for a few moments. I looked down at the stoop.

"Vincent, come here," my father said. "We need to talk."

"Oh shit," I mumbled under my breath. I got up, wiped my hands on my pants and walked toward my father.

"Let's go sit in the truck," he said.

I followed him to the truck. We got in and my father took a deep breath.

"Why don't you tell me what's going on?" he said.

"With what?"

"Vincent, let's not play games here. Tell me about you and his daughter Rachel."

"There's nothing to tell, dad."

"Not according to Mr. Levy. He told me that some neighbor of his saw you and Rachel necking or kissing or something up on Ocean Parkway by Avenue Z."

"That is such bullshit."

"You weren't kissing her?"

"No dad, I wasn't."

"Then what the hell was going on?"

I explained to my father exactly what was going on. Of course, I didn't tell him that I was falling in love with Rachel. I just told him the straight facts. That Rachel and I had talked a few times, had met on the bench by the bus stop at Avenue Z, that her father did not want her talking to me, and that we had just kissed each other on the cheeks last time we met. No big deal, or at least that's the way I tried to make it sound.

"Do you have feelings for this girl, Vincent?"

I could tell my father was uncomfortable asking me this.

"What do you mean?" I said.

"You know what I mean."

I just couldn't tell him the whole truth at that moment.

"Listen dad, we enjoy each other's company, we like talking to each other. I don't see what the big deal is, and I don't know why that would get Mr. Levy so mad."

My father took another deep breath. "Listen son, the Levys are Orthodox Jews. They are very religious. For their daughter to be involved with someone like you, well, they see it as a threat, I guess."

"A threat to what? Jesus, I just talked to her and we gave each other kisses on the cheek."

"Vincent, it's probably not a good idea to get involved with this girl. She's a pretty girl, I know, but the people over here on Ocean Parkway and in this neighborhood, well, it's like they live in a different world than we do. There's nothing wrong with that, but that's the way it is."

"This whole thing is just getting stupid," I said. "I talk to a girl, we become friends, we give each other a little kiss, and all of a sudden you have this big scandal going. What the hell is going on here?"

"Vincent, just listen to me. If, let's just say, you did become involved with this girl. On the surface there's nothing wrong with that, just two people who like each other. But there's a whole lot more involved, if you see what I mean. Obviously, Mr. Levy wants Rachel to date Jewish boys. And think about your mother. Mom is maybe even more Catholic than Mr. Levy is Jewish. The whole thing just seems like a recipe for disaster. The Levys are nice people, but I just can't see them coming to our house for macaroni on a Sunday. Do you understand what I'm trying to say?"

"Dad, let me ask you something. Your best friend in the army was Isaac Goldberg, right? He saved your life. I saw you cry when you talked about him. On top of that, he was Rachel's uncle."

My father looked at me with complete confusion on his face. I explained to him that Isaac's widow, who sat in our home all those years ago, was Mr. Levy's sister.

My father shook his head. "You know, you would think that if Levy knew that, he would have mentioned it to me when we were talking."

"He didn't say nothing?"

"Not a word about it."

"My point is this, dad. Isaac was like a brother to you. You're here today because of him. Did it matter that you were an Italian guy and he was a Jewish guy? Did he say on that beach, 'I'm not gonna help this guy cause he's a dago. And did you ever say, 'I'm not gonna watch out for this guy cause he's a Jew?'"

"That was different Vincent."

"Different how?"

"That was war. This is Brooklyn."

"What the hell does that mean?"

My father took a Lucky Strike out of the pack on the dashboard and lit it. I opened the window on my side to let the smoke out.

"War is just different," he said. "When you're out there, all that matters is surviving. You ain't fighting for some cause or to make the world free. That's what they tell you, and I guess in a bigger sense that's true, but when you're out there in combat the only reason you just don't get up and run away is because the guy next to you isn't running away. Believe me, every bone in your body is telling you to get the hell out of there. You watch out for each other. The guy next to you is all you have, and you're all he has. All you want to do is survive. All you want to do is live." He paused, took a long drag on his cigarette and exhaled. "All you want to do is live, and you'll kill to make sure you live."

My father had a distant, almost frightened look in his eyes. He stared out the front window of the truck as he spoke. He had never talked to me like this before. I doubted that he had ever talked to anybody like this before.

"That's why it's different," he continued. "On the battlefield are no differences between people. There are no rules. All the stuff we live with in our normal world is stripped away. It means nothing. You start every day hoping that it isn't your last day on earth. That's all you care about and that's all that matters. Then, if you're lucky enough to survive, you come home. And all the things that meant nothing on the battlefield all of a sudden mean something again. Do you understand what I'm saying?"

"I think so."

"Look Vincent, I'll give you an example. Suppose Mr. Levy fires us from this job because he doesn't want you around his daughter. Then he tells people in the neighborhood that they shouldn't hire me because my son has an eye for the Jewish girls. Next thing you know we lose thousands of dollars worth of work. That's the money that pays for our house and feeds us. You see the difference?"

My head was spinning. It was all too much. I was still trying to deal with what my father had told me about being in combat, let alone the difference between my situation and his friendship with Isaac Goldberg.

"Why the hell is everything so complicated?" I said.

"Vincent, the fact is, had my friend Isaac come home alive, we probably wouldn't have seen much of each other after the war, even though we lived a few blocks apart. He would have gone back to his world, and I would have gone back to mine, and those were two different worlds. Our friendship and our brotherhood would have always been there. And that meant a lot in Italy and France, but it wouldn't have meant a whole lot in Brooklyn."

"What the hell am I supposed to do now?"

"You really like this girl, don't you? This isn't just a casual friendship, is it?"

I looked at him but didn't answer. He knew by looking at me what the answer was.

"Son, I can't tell you how to live your life. You just gotta listen to your head sometimes and not your heart. Come on, we need to get back to work."

He got out of the truck but I sat there for a few more moments. Everything he had said made complete sense, but I didn't care. All I could think about was that I was supposed to meet Rachel at the bus stop at three o'clock. And I was going to meet her.

At a little before three I told my father I was taking my lunch break. He knew where I was going. He knew I had to talk to Rachel and nothing he said or did was going to stop me. As I walked past him he looked up and said, "Take as long as you need."

Rachel was torn as she rode home on the bus. Should she get off at Avenue Z and meet Vincent? What if her father had confronted Vincent and his father as he said he was going to do that day? Would Vincent even be there? And if he was, should she take the chance of being seen with him again? She wanted nothing more than to see Vincent. To see him smile as she walked towards him. She had to see him. Even in school that day her mind was a million miles away. All day she thought of Vincent, then she would think of the lecture her father had given her the night before. She thought of her own behavior and how, for the first time in her life, she had been defiant to her father. She felt bad about defying her father, but she also knew what she felt in her heart and at that moment it was all that mattered to her. She still wasn't sure what to do. If

Vincent were waiting on the bench when the bus stopped, she would decide what to do then. She would listen to her heart

---

I was on the bench on the corner of Avenue Z when the bus came to a stop. Rachel stepped off the bus but didn't come towards me. Instead she waved her hand for me to come to her. I ran to the bus door. Rachel grabbed me by the hand and pulled me on to the bus, dropping the change for my fare in the meter as we boarded. She led me to a seat in the back and we sat down. She sat by the window.

"What's this all about?" I asked.

"It wouldn't be a good idea to be seen at our bench again. Not after what my father told me last night."

"The shit hit the fan?"

"That's one way of putting it."

"Sorry, I shouldn't have cursed."

"That's okay. It kind of describes what happened. One of our neighbors saw us on the bench, and she saw me kiss you. She told my father and he kind of went nuts when I got home."

She held on to my hand. I squeezed it and she squeezed back. That magic electricity shot through me again. I had never thought it would be possible to feel so good just riding on a hot New York City bus.

"Did my father talk to your father this morning?" Rachel asked.

"Yeah, only it looked like your father did most of the talking."

"What happened?"

"I didn't hear what they were talking about, but after they were done my old man had a long talk with me in the truck."

"What'd he say?"

"He told me that your old man heard from a neighbor that we kissed each other by the bench, and that maybe it wasn't a good idea for me to get involved with a Jewish girl, that we come from different worlds. Stuff like that."

"I got the same lecture from my father last night."

"What the hell is everybody's problem? I mean, we've talked to each other three times and it seems like everybody's world is crumbling around them. For what? I just don't get it."

"They all think we're involved."

"Involved?"

"Yes, you know, like we want to be dating or be girlfriend and boyfriend."

"Do we?" I said. The words just came out of my mouth.

Rachel didn't answer me. She glanced out the window as the bus came to a stop to let people off. She turned back to me. I knew what I wanted to say to her. I wanted to tell her that our fathers were right about one thing. They were right about Mr. Levy's worst fear - that we did want to be "involved," that we were falling in love, that for me, and I knew for her as well, we were both feeling something neither of us had ever felt before. That's what I wanted to tell her. But I just couldn't get it out.

"Are we going to a Mets game?" she asked

"Do you think that's a good idea after all the stuff that's happened?"

"It's a great idea. What's wrong with two people going to a ballgame?"

"Absolutely nothing," I said.

"When?"

"Friday. The Mets play the Cubs. The game starts at seven. Walk to the Sheepshead Bay train station and I'll meet you there at about five o'clock. We'll take the train to the Polo Grounds from there."

We rode to the next stop in silence, still holding hands. We got off the bus, crossed the street, and waited for the bus going the other way. We boarded the bus when it came and not once did our hands come apart. As the bus approached the Avenue Z stop Rachel let go of my hand and stood up.

"You better let me get off first," she said, "and then give me a block head start before you follow. We don't need another Vincent and Rachel sighting. Not today."

"That sounds so good," I said.

"What?"

"Vincent and Rachel. It kinda goes together."

"I know," she said.

The bus stopped and we got off. I waited until she was about a block ahead of me before I started walking back to her house along the esplanade. It was a few minutes past four o'clock.

When I got back to the house my father was working on the stoop. He glanced up at me as I knelt to help him, but he didn't say anything. We worked until five then got in the truck to go home.

"You saw Rachel?" my father asked

"Yeah."

He started the truck and pulled out into traffic.

"Hey dad."

"Yeah."

"You know your friend, Mr. Ritigliano?"

"Yeah."

"He's got those season tickets to the Mets, you know, the ones right next to the Mets dugout at the Polo Grounds."

"Yeah, sure."

"Do you think you could get them for Friday night? I wanna go to a game. If you can't I'll just get other tickets, but those are pretty good seats."

"I'll call him when I get home. He doesn't use them all that much. It shouldn't be a problem."

"Good."

"Who you going to the game with?"

I was silent for a moment.

"A friend," I said.

I was going to a ball game Friday night.

CHAPTER SIX

Rachel was there at the Sheepshead Bay train station at five. She looked beautiful. She wore a dark blue dress with a pink shirt. I swear she took my breath away. Her long black hair blew in the breeze while we waited on the elevated train platform. The sun shone on her face and I thought to myself how I had never seen anyone look more beautiful in my life. I felt a little underdressed. I was wearing jeans, high top sneakers, a Mets tee shirt, a Mets jacket and a Mets hat. It was the way I always dressed when I went to a ballgame. I had a blanket with me because sometimes it got a little chilly at night games.

We took the train into Manhattan and then grabbed a northbound train to the Polo Grounds, which was way up on 154th street on the West Side. The first half of the ride uptown is underground, but as you get further north in Manhattan the train comes out of the tunnels and on to the elevated tracks that run along the east bank of the Hudson River. Rachel had never been that far uptown before. She stared out the window in amazement and awe at the city, the shining river and the coast of New Jersey. We held hands the entire way.

"You've never been up here before?" I asked.

"Vincent, I know my neighborhood, the area around my school and I've been to my father's office on West 43rd Street. That's about it. And in the summer, when I was a little girl, I used to go to summer camp in the Catskills."

I pointed out various sites and landmarks as we traveled uptown. She asked questions about everything. Finally the train pulled into the 154th Street station. We got off and I led her by the hand to the ballpark.

As we approached the stadium she looked up at it in wonder. "This is magnificent," she said.

There were thousands of people streaming toward the entrances. When we got inside I stopped at the souvenir stand and bought a program. We walked up the ramp and into the stands. When we emerged from the tunnel, the beautiful green field was spread out before us. Rachel stopped dead in her tracks and looked around.

"This is just so beautiful," she said. "The grass is so green and the dirt is so brown, and look at the colors of the uniforms the players are wearing. My God, it's so beautiful."

I smiled. Being with her and hearing her say those things reminded me of the first ballgame I went to at Ebbets Field in 1947. I had the same feelings and emotions she did. I've been to hundreds of games since then, but I always feel the same excitement when I emerge from the tunnel and see the beautiful green field spread out before me.

I led her to our seats, which were three rows from the field and just to the left of the Mets dugout on the first base side. I had sat there twice before when my father got tickets from Mr. Ritigliano, and they were incredible seats.

We were only a few feet from the field. We sat and watched the Mets take batting practice. I asked Rachel if she wanted something to eat or drink, but she told me that she was only allowed to eat kosher food. I wasn't sure exactly what that meant, but I figured I'd ask her another time. I got myself a bag of peanuts. Rachel had a few schoolbooks with her, because her father thought she was going to the Brooklyn Public Library to study. She put the books under her seat.

"Now there's one thing you gotta understand about the Mets," I said.

"And that is?"

"That they really stink. They're the worst team in baseball."

"Then why are you a Mets fan? I understand that the Yankees are good. They always seem to win."

"I could never root for the Yankees. Ever. I grew up a Brooklyn Dodger fan."

"And that means what?"

"It means I hate the Yankees."

"Why?"

"Okay. You see, in the Fifties, before the Dodgers went to Los Angeles, they were really good and they played the Yankees all the time in the World Series. The first five times they played the Yankees, they lost. They finally won the championship in 1955, but then lost again in the 1956 World Series. So they played the Yankees six times for the World Championship and lost five times. All Dodger fans hate the Yankees. I'm sure your father did."

"What does that have to do with the Mets?"

"Well, see, the Dodgers are in the National League and the Yankees are in the American League. You know about the two leagues?"

"Now I do."

"So all Dodger fans were National League fans. When they left Brooklyn we just couldn't start rooting for the Yankees in the other league, plus we all hate the Yankees, so we had no team to root for. Then the Mets started just this year, so now we have a team to root for again, even though they really stink. Did you get all that?"

"Yeah. I think so. But why are they so bad?"

"Well, when a new team starts, they get mostly the rejects from the other teams in the league. So, they're bound to stink. But that's okay. It makes it more fun when they win once and a while. Someday the Mets will be good. Just not right now."

"Are they going to win tonight?"

"I don't know. They have a chance. The Mets are in last place, but the Cubs aren't much better."

"And so they just have to score more points than the Cubs?"

"Runs. They have to score more runs."

"Okay, runs. Got it.

"Also, because we're so close to the field, you gotta watch out for foul balls."

"Got it."

"Do you know what a foul ball is?"

"One that isn't fair?"

"That's right."

"That was a wild guess."

"Well, sometimes a batter swings at a pitch, but doesn't hit it straight. He'll only get a part of the ball and it'll come flying into the stands really fast. So you have to be on your toes."

"Got it. Tell you what. If a foul ball comes toward us, you catch it, okay?

"Deal."

I can't even describe in words how wonderful it was to sit there with Rachel that night. It was an incredible feeling to see a whole new world open up to her. Up to that point, I had only seen her in her world. Now she was in mine. It was a beautiful night with a cool breeze blowing in from the outfield.

I pointed to the batting cage where the Mets were taking batting practice. "You see that big guy wearing number 14," I said.

"Yes."

"That's Gil Hodges. He was always my favorite player on the Dodgers. My father's, too. He plays first base in the field, which is over there," I pointed to the first base bag.

"Why isn't he still on the Dodgers?"

"Ah, well, he's getting kind of old for baseball, so the Dodgers sold him to the Mets so he could finish up his career in New York, where he played most of his career with the Dodgers. Besides, he lives on Bedford Avenue in Brooklyn. So when he came to the Mets he was coming home.

"How old is he?"

"He's thirty-six."

"That's not so old."

"It is for baseball."

Watching the game with Rachel that night was an amazing experience. Many things I took for granted as a baseball fan had to be explained to Rachel because she was a complete novice. It made me appreciate many things about the game that I had stopped taking notice of.

In the first inning a Cub batter hit a long fly ball to left field. It was basically a routine fly, but Rachel was mesmerized by it.

"That was amazing," she said. "How did that man in the outfield know exactly where that ball was going to come down?"

"He just judged it," I said.

"Can everybody who plays ball do that?"

"Sure, if you're halfway decent."

"Can you do that?"

"Sure I can. It becomes like second nature."

"Did you want to be a ballplayer?"

"More than anything. I was pretty good, just not good enough for the major leagues. Even the players on the Mets, the worst team in baseball, have to be incredible even to play in the big leagues."

The game turned into a pitcher's dual. The Cubs scored first on a home run by Ernie Banks, and then the Mets tied it in the fifth inning on a homer by Frank Thomas. When Thomas hit his homer the place went nuts. There were about 40,000 people there and Rachel got caught up in all the cheering. When the ball left the park over the right field wall, we both jumped up and screamed.

She was having the time of her life.

So was I.

It got a little chilly in the fifth inning, so we got under the blanket and held each other's hand. I had never been more content or happy in my life.

Another thing that fascinated Rachel was how fast the pitchers threw the ball.

"How can they possibly make the ball go that fast?" she said over and over again. "And how can the batter possibly hit it?"

"Because they're big leaguers. And that's not all. Sometimes the ball curves, or dips. And sometimes it comes right at you and you gotta get outta the way."

"How fast do they throw?"

"Between eighty-five and ninety miles-an-hour. Some guys throw even faster. In fact, Sandy Koufax on the Dodgers throws about ninety-five. He's the best pitcher in the game. And you know something else? He's a Jewish kid from Brooklyn."

"I wonder if my father knows that."

"I'm sure he does."

In the bottom of the ninth the game was still tied at one. With one out the Met shortstop, Elio Chacon, got a double and after the second out was made, Gil Hodges stepped to the plate. Everybody in the place was standing. They cheered loudly as Gil took his practice swings.

"Okay, let me explain this to you," I said to Rachel. "The home team always gets last licks."

"They get what?"

"Last licks. The Polo Grounds here is the Mets home field. That means in the bottom of the last inning, the ninth, they get the last turn at bat. If they are losing and the other team gets them out, they lose the game. But, if it's tied, like it is now, and they score a run. They win automatically. The game is over."

"What if it ends in a tie?"

"Baseball never ends in a tie. You keep playing until one team wins."

"So if the Mets score now they win the game?"

"That's right. You're a natural at this."

"I have a good teacher."

Gil Hodges took the first pitch for a ball, then fouled off the second pitch for a strike.

"Come on Mr. Hodges!" Rachel yelled. "Hit a good one!"

I looked at her.

"Did I say something wrong?" she asked.

"No, it was perfect."

On the next pitch Gil hit a ground ball up the middle. It went past the pitcher and somehow found its way between the shortstop and second baseman. By the time it rolled into the outfield, Elio Chacon had scored and the Mets won one of only 42 games they would win that year.

The ballpark erupted in cheering. Rachel and I joined in and started jumping up and down. At one point we just turned toward each other and I threw my arms around her. She did the same to me. We stopped jumping and I looked down at her.

We held each other very tightly. She felt perfect in my arms. She picked her head up and looked at me and I kissed her. That magical electricity shot through my body. It was a long kiss and the noise in the ballpark just faded into the background. When we finally parted I looked into her eyes and they were shining.

"I've been waiting two weeks to do that," I said. "Since the first time I saw you."

"I know."

We kissed again. It was, to that point in my life, the greatest feeling I had ever experienced. How could anybody think what we felt for each other was so wrong, when we both knew it was so right?

We sat down and I put the blanket over us. We looked around at over 40,000 people cheering. It felt like they were cheering for us. It was such a sweet spot in time that neither one of us wanted it to end. But we had to leave to make sure Rachel got home on time. The last thing we needed was another scene with her father.

On the train ride home we sat cuddled together. I had my arm around her and we kissed each other most of the way. When we changed trains and got the train back to Brooklyn, it was about ten o'clock and there were only a few other people in our car. A couple of stops before our stop, a drunken wino came staggering on to the train and started panhandling for change. He worked his way toward us and stopped in front of me.

"Hey buddy," he said, "you gotta nickel or dime? I need to get shumtin' to eat."

He smelled horribly. He looked to be in his thirties, and from his bent nose and scarred hands, I thought to myself that at one point he must have been a prizefighter. I gave him a dime. "Move on buddy," I said.

Instead, he turned to Rachel.

"What about you lady? You got some change so I can eat shumtin'?"

"Hey buddy," I said, leaning over, "I told you to move on."

"I was just askin' the lady for some change."

"I gave you some change. Beat it."

He ignored me and leaned closer to Rachel. She cringed at his odor. That was it. I got up, grabbed him by the shirt, and pushed him across the train car, pinning him against the seat opposite us.

"I told you to beat it," I said. "I gave you some change, now it's time to leave."

He struggled against my grip, and he was no weakling. Still, I held on tight and pushed him toward the end of the car. I opened the door at the end of the car, went out between the cars with him, then opened the door to the next car and pushed him into it.

"Don't come back," I said.

I closed the door and went back into our car and sat down next to Rachel.

"Sorry about that," I said.

"About what, Vincent?"

"About that wino bothering you."

"He smelled bad, but I wasn't worried. I knew you'd protect me."

I smiled then looked down at the floor. "My father always says you have to protect the people you love."

"Well then, I have to protect you, too" she said softly.

"You have to protect me?"

"Like you said, you protect the people you love."

"So, I guess that means we love each other."

"You don't know that by now?"

"I knew it all along," I said. "I just wasn't sure if you felt the same way."

"I knew that you knew and you knew that I knew, so we both knew. We just didn't know how to say what we knew." She paused, then said, "Did that make any sense?"

"It made complete sense."

I kissed her again.

The wino didn't come back and we got off at our station at around ten-thirty or so.

I walked with Rachel until we were about a block from her house. We held hands the entire way. We figured since it was dark out, there wouldn't be any nosy neighbors around.

"I better go alone from here," she said. "Don't want my dad seeing us."

"I know."

"How much longer are you going to be working at my house?"

"Maybe a few more days. We're almost done."

"Oh shit, that's no good."

"Rachel! Jeez! I never thought I'd hear that word come out of your mouth."

"That's cause you're a bad influence on me."

"Come on, not that bad."

"Okay, just a little."

"Sometimes it feels good to be bad."

"I know, I'm just finding that out."

"What are we gonna do, Rachel?"

"I'm not sure, Vincent."

"Either am I. I just know that I gotta see you."

"Look, tomorrow is Saturday. We get out of temple about twelve, then we just hang around on the esplanade for a few hours in the afternoon. Meet me down by the entrance to Prospect Park about one o'clock. I'll just go for a walk and meet you at the park."

"You know I'll be there."

"We can spend a couple of hours together and try and figure this thing out. I have to go, it's getting late."

I gathered her in my arms and kissed her. It felt like she just melted into me.

"Rachel," I said, "I think I love you."

"You just think that?"

"No, I know that. I was never so sure of anything in my life."

"I love you, Vincent."

"You better get going. I'll watch from here until you get in your front door."

"I know you will. You protect the things you love."

It was Saturday afternoon and the Levys were out on the esplanade in front of their house. Mr. Levy had suspected nothing the night before, so Rachel felt relieved. Saturday afternoons, after temple, were a time for socializing and it was a beautiful early fall day. There was a slight breeze in the trees and the traffic on Ocean Parkway was light.

Mr. Levy sat on a bench with his next door neighbor, Manny Dranoff, who was a furrier. Rachel sat next to her father on the other side.

"So Henry," said Mr. Dranoff. "Did you hear about the Mets game last night? They won it in the ninth. Our old friend Gil Hodges got the game-winning hit."

"I don't follow baseball anymore," Mr. Levy replied. "Ever since the Dodgers left Brooklyn, I have no interest. Besides, the Mets stink."

Rachel stood up and looked at her father. "But dad, you were a Dodger fan. That means you must have hated the Yankees because they beat Brooklyn in the World Series all those times, except 1955. You should now be a Mets fan. It's the National League, after all. And they have Gil Hodges, who was a great Dodger."

Henry Levy stared at his daughter in stunned silence.

"I'm going to take a walk," said Rachel. "It's such a beautiful day." She turned and headed up the esplanade toward Prospect Park.

"Rachel," her father called after her, "come back here a moment."

Rachel looked back over her shoulder at her father. "I'll be back in a couple of hours. I think Sandy Koufax is pitching for the Dodgers tonight. You know, dad, he's a nice Jewish boy from Brooklyn."

CHAPTER SEVEN

Rachel and I sat on a bench in Prospect Park. In our short romance we had met on the walkway in front of her house, two benches on Ocean Parkway, a bus, and went to a ball game. Definitely not the stuff of great romance movies. The day was cool and fall was in the air. We were trying to figure out how to see each other as much as possible. We talked for about an hour and got nowhere. She insisted that her father could not, under any circumstances, find out about our relationship, not for the time being anyway. We were both frustrated, and I was getting impatient and irritated. I told her I would feel like a fool running around hiding from her father.

"So what are we gonna do?" I asked.

"I don't know, Vincent."

"Look, why can't we just tell your father we're seeing each other? You're gonna be twenty. You should be able to do what you want."

She looked down. "It isn't that easy. Not for me. Just the thought of my not seeing a Jewish boy would drive my father crazy."

"Why? What's the matter with the rest of us?"

"It's not that. It's just, well, tradition I guess, or whatever you want to call it."

"That's bullshit if you ask me."

" What, tradition?"

"No Rachel, not tradition. I'm a wop, we got nothing but traditions. It's the fact that I'm not Jewish so I'm not good enough for you."

"That's not it at all, Vincent."

I could tell by her tone of voice she was a bit perturbed at me, but I was getting pretty pissed off myself.

"Then what exactly is it?" I said. "He doesn't want you to be romantically involved with anyone but a Jew. End of story. So it's that whole chosen people thing again. The rest of us aren't chosen so we're just second class human beings, not worthy of falling in love with a Jew. What crap."

"I wish you wouldn't curse."

"Saying crap isn't cursing," I said. "Saying bullshit is cursing, and that's what I think this is."

We sat in silence for a moment. There just didn't seem to be a way out of the whole dilemma.

"Look," I said, "a person doesn't decide who he or she is going to fall in love with. It just happens. Believe me, when we started the job at your house the last thing I ever thought was that in a very short time I'd fall in love with an Orthodox Jewish girl and have to deal with all this stuff."

"Either did I. I don't think I've ever really been in love before. Have you?"

I ran my hand through my hair. I didn't want to say the wrong thing.

"I thought maybe I was," I answered. "You know, I had girlfriends in high school and one afterwards, but

I never felt about any of them the way I feel about you. It's just a whole other thing."

"It's a new thing for me. I mean, I've dated before and I guess I had some crushes on some guys, but I never felt anything like this."

"Me neither. Look Rachel, there's got to be a way to do this. What? Are we just going to sneak around all the time?"

She exhaled heavily, it seemed to me in frustration.

"Well, is that what you think?" I said. "That we got to sneak around?"

"I don't think there's any other way right now. I'll know when it's the right time to tell my father. Just not now."

"You got to be kidding."

"I'm not."

"How are we going to do this? I work, you go to school, when the hell are we going to get to see each other?"

"We'll figure something out."

"Yeah, like what?"

"I don't know Vincent, but we can."

"Jesus Christ."

"We have Saturdays and Sundays. After temple on Saturday, I have the day to myself. What about Sunday?"

"I don't go to church anymore. Not since I started working full time with my old man. That really gets my mother mad, but I work hard all week and I hate having to get up early on a Sunday."

"You can get away with that?"

"What? Not going to church?"

"Yes."

"Sure, I'm twenty-one. I went to church almost every Sunday of my life until I started working. I can make my own choices now."

"I can't."

"What, make your own choices?"

"As long as I live under my father's roof, I have to obey his rules."

"But you're a grown woman."

"Not according to my father."

"So, you're going to finish school, then take over the finances of your father's whole company, but you're not grown up enough to make your own decisions about who you're going to be in love with? Does that make sense to you?"

"I didn't say it made sense. I just said that's the way it is."

"The way it is? That's all you can say?"

"What else am I supposed to do? Go against my father? Just by seeing you and being here now I'm going against him."

All I could do was just shake my head. My parents were always strict, but I couldn't imagine them being so rigid.

"Don't you have rules in your house?" she asked.

"I have rules, sure. And to tell you the truth, I'm pretty sure my mother isn't going to be too happy that I'm seeing a Jewish girl. She's a real strict Catholic. She'll be upset, she'll try and talk me out of it. But she'd never forbid me to do it."

"Well, it isn't that easy with my father."

"What about your mother?"

"I think she would prefer I see a Jewish boy, too, but I don't think she'd be upset as my father."

"So this all comes down to your father being mad because I'm not a Jew?"

"He's not mad, as you say, cause you're not a Jew. He just wants me to date Jewish boys. Vincent, we come from very different backgrounds, and it could be very difficult. I guess my father just doesn't want to see get me hurt."

I stood up and started to pace up and down in front of the bench. I was frustrated and I was getting mad.

"Vincent, it's not that much different than if we could let my father know," she said

"What are you taking about?"

"You said it. You work and I go to school, so we'd only be able to probably see each other on the weekends anyway."

"No, that isn't true. If we didn't have to keep everything from your old man, I could call you on the phone. Maybe we could have a cup of coffee at a diner after work or school. Maybe I could drop by at night at your house for an hour after dinner, or you could come by my house. That would be normal."

"I could do that?"

"Do what?"

"Come by your house at night?"

"Well, yeah, I guess. I'd have to prepare my mother a little. But, yeah, everybody is welcome at my house. It's always like that. You come in, you eat, that's the way it is with Italians."

"Even for an Orthodox Jewish girl who's in love with an Italian boy?"

"Yeah, of course," I said, but I knew I'd have to have a little talk with my mother first. She wasn't a prejudiced woman at all. But she was very religious, and the thought of her son being romantically involved with a Jew would definitely disturb her. I knew that. But I also knew that, in the end, if it made me happy, she'd deal with it.

"You don't sound so sure," Rachel said.

"I am," I answered.

"Well, it's just not that way with my father. I just think with him, he can't find out right away. You know, he got all upset just by me talking to you."

"That's crazy."

"You don't understand."

"What, am I an idiot? What's not to understand?"

"He's just old-fashioned when it comes to stuff like this."

"Oh, is that what old-fashioned means?" I said sarcastically. "Somebody thinks somebody else is not as good as they are because they ain't the same religion?"

"I didn't say that. And that's not what he thinks. He respects everybody."

"Sure don't sound that way to me."

"Vincent, I don't think there's any other way we can see each other right now, unless we keep it from him for a while. I need to have a little time. I'm just trying to see if we can figure this out for now. Obviously I'm going to have to tell my father about us at some point. But I have to wait until I think the time is right. I have to talk to my mom first, and then we'll both talk to my dad. Or something like that."

"You know what? I don't think that's such a good idea, Rachel. I've known you two weeks, we've been together like five times, and you know something, I love you. That by itself is pretty amazing. But I'll be damned if I'm going to sneak around like some fool because you're old man thinks I'm a lower form of life because I ain't a Jew."

"He doesn't think you're a lower form of life."

"I don't see what else it is."

"Vincent, all we need to do is give it a little time. I can't just go barging into my father and tell him I'm in love with you. That would really be the end of it. I never told him I was in love with anybody, let alone a goy.

"Let him think what he wants. I don't give a shit."

"Vincent, please."

"Okay, I don't give a crap. Is that better?"

"You don't have to be sarcastic."

"Well, I can't help being a wise-ass. It's in my blood."

"That doesn't help the situation."

I looked at Rachel and she raised her eyes up to meet mine. I loved her for sure, but I was angry. I just couldn't come to grips with the fact that her father saw me as some type of lowlife for not being Jewish. At least that's the way it felt. No matter how much I loved this girl, I just didn't think I could sneak around like a fool with something to hide.

"Rachel, listen to me. You got some serious thinking to do. You understand? I'm not going to play games. I love you, but no matter how I feel about you, you have to deal with your own situation. I can't tell you what to do. You have to decide for yourself. I'll tell you one thing, though, if you think I'm going to sneak around to see you to avoid your father getting all pissed off, I don't know if I can do that. Maybe I have so far, but I'm not sure how long I can keep doing it."

"Then that's it then?

"What's it?"

"If I don't go marching into my house and tell my father about us, you're just going to throw this whole thing away?"

"I didn't say exactly that."

She stood up.

"Then what the hell did you say?" she said.

For a moment I was taken aback just by Rachel using the word "hell." Then I felt the anger and frustration rising in me again.

"It ain't my decision. It's yours."

"Fine."

"Fine."

We stood staring at each other. Neither one of us had anything to say.

"I got to go," I said. "I'm supposed to meet some of my friends to play handball. At least they don't look down on me. Then again, they're lowlife Italians, too. They weren't lucky enough to be born one of the chosen people."

"You are a real wise-ass, aren't you?"

"Just telling the truth."

"Everybody's truth is different."

"Yeah, I'm finding that out."

"So am I."

"Fine, I got to go," I said, then I added sarcastically, "Tell your father I said hello."

I walked off toward Ocean Parkway and left her standing there.

I didn't look back.

Rachel didn't think it was possible to feel as bad as she did. She had a horrible, empty feeling in the pit of her stomach.

As she approached her house she saw that her parents and brothers were still out on the esplanade socializing, but she went into the house and up to her bedroom. She sat on her bed and thought about the fight she had just had with Vincent. She knew in her heart he was right, but she also knew it just wasn't the right time to tell her father about them. She wasn't sure when that time would come, she just knew it wasn't then.

She had never in her life felt so many emotions at once. She felt hurt, anger, confusion and sadness. Is this what love is all about?

At dinner that night Rachel just picked at her food. Her mother kept looking at her. Mrs. Levy knew something was bothering Rachel. She asked Rachel once or twice if she was feeling okay, and Rachel told her that she was just tired, but Mrs. Levy knew better.

Rachel went to bed at about nine o'clock but couldn't fall asleep. She just lay in bed staring at the ceiling. Is it over? she thought. Will I ever see Vincent again ? Is this it?

Her parents climbed the steps to come to bed at about ten o'clock. Her mother said something to her father, and then Rachel heard her walking down the hallway. She knocked on Rachel's door softly.

"Rachel?"

"Yeah Mom?"

"Can I come in?"

"Yeah."

Rachel sat up in bed and her mother sat next to her.

"Rachel, what's on your mind today? Mrs. Levy asked. "You're just not yourself."

"I'm okay."

"I know better than that. There is something troubling you."

Rachel couldn't tell her about her fight with Vincent, so she made something up.

"I guess it's just a lot of things," she said. "School is hard. I have a lot of tests coming up. Plus, I've been thinking about my trip to Israel after I finish school, then working for Dad. It's a little overwhelming, I guess. I know it's a year away, but time seems to be moving so fast."

"Rachel, you're growing up now. These are the responsibilities you're going to have. They never seemed to bother you before."

"Yeah, I know, but now everything's getting closer

day by day and it's a little scary."

They sat in silence for a moment. Her mother brushed the hair from Rachel's face.

"There's something else on your mind, Rachel, isn't there?

"No mom, I'm okay.

"Is it that Italian boy who's working here?"

Rachel looked up at her quickly. Does she know something? she thought. Does she know I have been seeing Vincent? How can she know?

"What does that have to do with it?" asked Rachel.

"Rachel, you are my daughter. I know you. I know your moods. I know when you are happy or sad or frustrated. I can see it in you. These past two weeks I have seen a change in you. It's nothing I can exactly put my finger on, but there is something. There is a glow about you, a happiness and excitement I have never seen in you before."

"That's not true, Mom, I……

"Yes it is Rachel. I can see it in you. Is it the boy?"

She knows, Rachel thought. She looked at her mother and nodded her head, then sat back on her pillow and exhaled heavily.

"Please don't tell dad," said Rachel. "Not yet."

"How often have you seen him?"

"I've met him at the bus stop a few times, and we went to a baseball game together."

"A baseball game? When?"

"Last night. You and dad thought I was at the library. We went to see the Mets play."

"Did you have fun?"

"Mom, I had the best time of my life. Please don't tell dad."

"I won't say anything. Are you sure you're doing the right thing?"

"I don't know if it's right or wrong or anything. All I know is that I have never felt this way before."

"You do understand Rachel that if you continue to see this boy, it could be very difficult."

"I know. But what should I do? I can't help the way I feel. When I'm with him, when I just see him, well, it just feels wonderful."

Mrs. Levy shook her head and smiled.

"What, Mom?"

"I understand. We do not choose who we fall in love with. Sometimes it just happens."

"Vincent said that today."

"You saw him today?"

"Yes, we met in the park."

"What did you do?"

Rachel paused. "We just talked…and we had a fight."

"About what?"

"He's upset that I can't tell dad about us. He doesn't want to have to sneak around so we can see each other. He walked away today and I don't know if he wants to see me anymore. I guess he's right, but I don't think I can tell dad, not right now anyway."

"Rachel, as I said, it will be difficult. You and this boy come from two very different worlds. And your father, well, you know he is very strict in what he believes."

"Vincent thinks dad looks down on him because he's not Jewish."

"You know better than that, Rachel. Your father has respect for everybody. But yes, he is very old-fashioned. He wants what's best for you."

"How does he know what's best for me?"

"Rachel, we are very strict Orthodox Jews, your father most of all. You understand that a relationship between you and a Catholic boy will have many difficulties you can't even imagine. Your father doesn't want to see you get hurt. I don't either. And the chances are that the differences between you and this boy Vincent will cause nothing but hurt. Can you see that?"

"I guess," said Rachel. "But we can try. Maybe it will work out. No one knows the future. Dad says that all the time."

Her mother leaned forward and kissed Rachel on the forehead. As she sat back Rachel glanced down at the blue numbers tattooed on her mother's right forearm and then quickly looked way. Mrs. Levy saw Rachel's glance and looked down at her arm. She lightly rubbed the numbers with her left hand.

"These are my lucky numbers," she said softly.

Rachel was shocked by this statement. "Mom, those are the numbers they put on you in the camp. How can you say they are lucky?"

"I am lucky, Rachel. I survived. I have a wonderful husband and three beautiful children. I live free in America. And look at this." She pointed to the four numbers. "Add them up."

Rachel read the number - 6875. It added up to 26. "It's 26, mom," she said

"And what is your birthday"

"February 26th."

"You see, it's the day you were born, two-six. That was the happiest day of my life. After what I had been through, to give life to another who was mine. A baby girl who would grow up free in America, it was a miracle."

Rachel couldn't believe what she was hearing. Yet from the glow on her mother's face she knew her mother really believed in what she said.

"What happened in the camp, mom?"

Mrs. Levy looked down, and then looked up into Rachel's eyes. "It is nothing you should hear about."

"But it is, mom. It is part of you, so it is part of me, and it is part of my heritage. I have always wanted to know, but you have never talked about it."

"It is not a pleasant thing to speak of, and it is not something I have ever wanted my children to hear."

"Please mom, I need to know. I have always wanted to know."

"Rachel, I have never even told your father about all my experiences in the camp. Before we were married I wanted to tell him. I thought it was his right to know. But he wouldn't let me. He told me that I was his beautiful Anna, and what had happened in the camp made no difference. He promised me we would be married and raise a family and have a wonderful life in America, and that's all that mattered. And your father has given me everything he ever promised."

"I still want to know, mom.

"Rachel, I have never told anyone."

"But tell me, your daughter."

"I am not so sure you will want to hear it."

"I have read books. I have learned about it. I want to know what happened to you and how you survived."

Her mother looked toward the window in Rachel's room for a long while, staring into the darkness outside. It seemed to Rachel as if she was seeing images in her mind. There was pain on her face and in her eyes. Maybe, Rachel thought, I shouldn't have insisted she tell me.

"Mom, if you really don't want….."

"You are a grown woman now, Rachel. If you want to know I will tell you. This goes no further than this room. And I will hold nothing back. I will tell you everything. There are some things I did that I'm sure will make you ashamed of me."

"There is nothing that can make me ashamed of you," said Rachel.

"Rachel, you have not heard what I have to say yet. I know you have asked me about my time in the camp many times. I will tell you now, and as I said, I will tell you everything. Are you sure of this?"

"Yes, I am."

"What I tell you goes no further than this room. Not to your father or your brothers, even if they ask you."

"I understand."

"The Germans came into Poland in 1939," she began. "They did not come for us until early 1940. We lived in a small farming village. We were not farmers. My father, your grandfather Josef, had a small dry goods store in town. Our house was up the block from the store. I was eighteen then, my older brother, Karol, was twenty-one and worked with my father at the store. Your grandmother, Emily, was a beautiful woman. You look very much like her.

"The Germans came in the middle of the night. There were six soldiers. They broke down the door when we were all asleep. When we all ran into the kitchen to see what the loud noises were, the soldiers pointed their rifles at us. My father started to yell at them, and just like that a soldier took a bayonet from his belt and stabbed my father in the chest. My mother and I screamed. My father fell to the floor. My mother ran to him and knelt down beside him. Then another soldier hit her in the head with the butt of his rifle. When my brother saw this, he jumped on the soldier. Two other soldiers grabbed my brother and dragged him outside. Then I heard gun shots."

Mrs. Levy stopped to compose herself. She took a deep breath and looked at Rachel.

"Are you sure you want to hear more?" she asked her daughter.

"Tell me, mom."

"They took my mother and me from our home and left your grandfather dead on the floor. I don't remember much of the next few hours. I guess I was in shock. As we walked outside, I saw my brother's body lying in the yard. The next thing I remember was that we were at the train station. There were hundreds of people there. All the Jews in our town. Then they put us on the train. We were packed into empty cattle cars. People were screaming, children were crying. The men who protested were shot on the spot. There were so many people packed into our train car that it was difficult to breathe. My dear mother was delirious. She had a bleeding wound on her head from where the soldier had hit her with the rifle. She kept calling out for my father and my brother. She kept asking where they were."

"What did you tell her?" asked Rachel.

"I think I told her they were working at the store, but it's difficult to remember."

Anna Levy took another deep breath and continued.

"I don't know how many hours we were on the train. But it was a very, very long time. All I knew is that we were headed east. People had to, you know, go to the bathroom, and they relieved themselves right there in the train car. The smell was unbearable. It was pitch black when they shut the door of the train car, but some people had matches and lit them. The people saw that my mother was bleeding badly, and somehow they made room for me to sit down and for my mother to lay down with her head on my lap. I had to sit in urine and feces, and your grandmother was lying in it. She kept asking for my father and brother, then she finally fell asleep. I thought she was asleep, but soon her body got cold and I realized she had died. Perhaps the soldier who hit her with the rifle had cracked her skull. I don't know. She died in my arms, lying in a pool of human waste."

"Oh my God," said Rachel. It just came out.

"I have never told anyone of this, Rachel. I will stop if you want."

"No mom, I have read about these things. It just hurts to think of it happening to you."

"For most of the many hours on the train, there was a baby crying in the car. Then the baby just stopped. When we arrived at the camp the soldiers opened the doors to our cars. It was morning. The bright sunlight hurt our eyes. When they opened the door and the light came in, I noticed that your grandmother still had her gold wedding band and diamond engagement ring on her finger, and a gold necklace my father had given her around her neck. I knew the Germans would take these. I am a little ashamed of what I did next, but I took the rings off her fingers and the necklace off her neck, and then I reached under my dress and hid them in myself."

"What do you mean?"

"Rachel, I hid them in the only place possible. The only place I could. In a place only a woman has. I did not want the Germans to have them. They were given to my mother by my father."

Rachel didn't know what to say to her mother. What could she say?

Her mother continued. "The people spilled off the trains. Many were dragged off, dead. They dragged your grandmother out of our car, and dragged her body across the yard to a building. It was the last time I ever saw her. I found out later that the building they took her to was the crematorium where they burned many bodies.

"When the young woman with the baby got off the train we could all see that the baby was dead. The German soldiers saw this, too. They went up to the woman and tried to rip the dead child from her arms. She wouldn't let go. Finally, a soldier stabbed her in the back with a bayonet. She fell dead to the ground and the baby fell from her arms. Another soldier speared the dead baby with his bayonet, then walked across the yard and dumped it in a trashcan. The other soldiers laughed as he did this. I glanced over and saw the dead baby's foot sticking out of the trash barrel. Even to this day, there are times when I see a trash barrel on the street and I have to turn away. In my mind I can still see that child's foot.

"The men were separated from the women and we were herded into wooden cabins. They had dirt floors, at least mine did. That night, when everybody was asleep, I took your grandmother's jewelry from inside me and buried it in the dirt under my wooden cot. I didn't know what I was going to do with it, but it was all I had left of my family, and I did not want the Germans to take these things away.

"The next morning two officers came into our cabin and made us all stand up. They pointed to me and a soldier grabbed me by the arm and led me out. They took me to the house of the commandant of the camp. He needed a housekeeper and a cook. I was young and attractive and I guess the other officers thought the commandant would like me. The commandant's name was Colonel Edwin Schultz. For the first week he didn't seem to pay much attention to me. His wife was there visiting him and I just did my job.

"Everyday I saw hundreds of people herded into the gas chambers as I walked to the commandant's house. They buried the bodies on the grounds outside the camp. They made the prisoners dig huge ditches, and then throw the bodies in by the hundreds. Some bodies they burned in the crematorium. I don't know why they buried some bodies and burned others. They just did. When they burned bodies, the ashes would come out of the smokestacks and float down on the camp like snow. Even now, in the winter when it snows, I am reminded of that."

Mrs. Levy turned toward the bedroom window again and stared out into the darkness. She turned back to Rachel, started to say something, and then looked out the window again.

"What is it, mom?" asked Rachel.

Her mother turned toward her slowly. "Rachel," she said softly, "please do not be ashamed of me for what I am about to tell you."

"Mom, I told you, there is nothing that could make me ashamed of you. Nothing."

Mrs. Levy swallowed hard. "One night, after my first week working at the colonel's house, his wife left to return to Germany. That night he was drinking heavily. As I went to the door to leave he stopped me. He grabbed me by the arm and spun me around. He said something in German and started to kiss me. I tried to resist him, but he was very strong and slapped me and punched me again and again. I could not stop him. Do I have to say what happened next, Rachel?"

Rachel couldn't speak. She looked into her mother's eyes through her own tears. Her mother was not crying, but had a haunted look on her face that Rachel had never seen before.

"The colonel had his way with me every night for the two weeks that followed, until his wife returned. I prayed for her return every night. At first I tried to fight him, but he was too strong. After the first few nights I just let him do what he wanted to me. I lay there like a dead person. If I fought him he would have beaten me up, and I was afraid he might kill me in a drunken rage."

Mrs. Levy paused for a long moment, then continued.

"Rachel, I am about to tell you something I have kept inside me all these years. Your father doesn't know. No one knows." She looked directly into her daughter's eyes. "Rachel, if she is alive, you and your brothers have a sister somewhere in Europe."

At first Rachel was not sure exactly what her mother meant. She was so overcome with emotion that her mother's words did not immediately have meaning to her. Then, after a moment, Rachel understood. Her mother saw the realization on her face.

"When I missed my period the first month, I thought maybe it was because I hadn't been eating well, or was sick. But when I missed it for a second month, I knew I was pregnant with the colonel's child.

I worked at the colonel's house for about four months until my pregnancy began to show. When the baby started to show in my stomach, the colonel told me that the sight of a pregnant Jew sickened him, and he threw me out of his house. I was then put on a work detail cleaning the outhouses in the camp. To this day I don't know how my baby survived. I had little to eat and was worked ten hours a day.

"On the day the baby was born I was in the infirmary with the German doctors. The whole time I was pregnant I remember thinking that I wanted to hate this baby. It was the offspring of a monster who raped me. But as it grew inside of me I came to love it. The baby was mine. I was giving it life like I gave you and your brothers life. Yet sometimes, at night, I would hope that the baby died inside me so it didn't have to be born into the horrible world I lived in.

"As soon as the baby was born the German doctors took it away. When they held it up, I could see it was a girl. I never even got to hold her. I never actually saw her face. In my mind, I named her Emily, after my mother. A week or two later, I can't recall exactly, I was sent back to work in the colonel's house. When his wife was not there he continued to have his way with me. I decided that I had to escape or die trying.

"There was a laundry truck that came to the colonel's house once a week. I knew if I could get on that truck, I could jump off when it left the camp. I had no idea where I was going to go, but I knew I had to escape. I would have rather died or been shot than have the colonel rape me every night.

"I knew what days the truck came. It was my job to bring the laundry to the truck. The nights before the truck came, I would dig up your grandmother's jewelry and hide it in myself. But I did not put it in the women's place. I put it in the other place. I did not want the colonel to find it if his wife was not there and he assaulted me again. I knew if I escaped I could trade or sell the jewelry for food and clothes, or perhaps use it as a bribe.

"One day, by what can only be a miracle from God, I had my chance. The driver of the truck went inside. I looked around and there was no one in sight. I climbed into the truck and hid under the dirty clothes and sheets. When the truck was a few miles from camp, I jumped out of the back.

"I knew I had to move fast because it wouldn't be long before the colonel discovered I was missing. I didn't know exactly where in Poland I was, but I started walking west because I knew we had traveled east coming to the camp. I slept in fields, barns and churches. I stole food from farmhouses when the families were working in the fields. There were times I went for many days without eating. Fortunately, it was springtime, so the weather was warm, but it rained often, and I spent many nights soaking wet when I could not find shelter. I honestly had no idea where I was headed. I just kept going west to get as far away from Poland and the camp as I could. I ate vegetables from the farm fields. I stole food and clothes from farmhouses. A few times a farmer would find me sleeping in his barn. Fortunately, I was lucky. These farmers hated the Nazis as much as I did, so they fed and clothed me, and hid me in their hay carts so I could ride instead of walk to the next town. I made my way through Czechoslovakia and southern Germany. I was hoping to perhaps meet members of the secret resistance. Despite all the walking and hiding as I went, I began to feel stronger. On my trek across Europe I ate better than I had in the camp.

"In Germany a farmer discovered me in his house stealing food. It was on that day your grandmother Emily saved my life. The farmer started screaming at me. I had your grandmother's jewelry in a pouch under my dress. I reached into the pouch and pulled out the two rings and offered them to the farmer. I kept the necklace in the pouch. He took the rings from my hand and yelled at me to leave, pointing to the door. I grabbed a loaf of bread as I left. If not for me bribing him with the rings, I am sure he would have turned me in to the authorities, and I would have been shot or sent back to the camps.

"It took me many, many weeks, I have no idea how long, but somehow I made it to France. The Germans were in France, too, but I came to a small French farming village where not many German soldiers were stationed. I came to a farm and went into the barn and fell asleep in the hay. I was awakened by the farmer a few hours later. I thought he would tell the Germans I was there and I would be arrested and executed. At that time I was so tired and so desperate I didn't care what they did with me. I was lucky. The farmer and his wife were kind people who hated the Nazis.

"The farmer's wife took me in and nursed me back to health. Her name was Yvette Gagnon. Her husband's name was Henri. They had no children. We had a difficult time understanding each other. I spoke no French and they knew no Polish. Somehow, with hand gestures and looking at maps, I communicated to them that I had somehow arrived at their farm after escaping from a concentration camp in Poland. I also communicated to them what had happened to my family. I remember that both cried when they came to understand that the Germans murdered my family.

"This is the only part of my story that your father knows. He knows of my stay at the Gagnon farm because once or twice a year I get a letter from Mrs. Gagnon. Your father saw one of her letters from France that I received after the war and asked who it was from. All I told him was that it was from the French family that took me in and took care of me after I escaped from the camp. I told him that I owed the Gagnons my life. Your father just nodded when I told him this. I was going to tell him more, but he held his hand up to stop me. He once again told me that I did not have to tell him anything if I didn't want to. If the memories caused me pain, there was no reason for me to remember or relive that pain. I never said anything else about it to him."

"I have seen those letters from France," said Rachel. "I've always wondered what they were. They are written in French, how do you read them?"

"The man who owns the dry cleaning store on Avenue S is a French Canadian Jew. He translates them for me. You know, after the war I often wondered if the Gagnons had survived. I wrote to the town hall in their little town to get their address and sent them my first letter about a year after the war ended. Mrs. Gagnon was thrilled to hear from me, and was so happy that I had made it to America. Her husband, Henri, died right after the war ended. She hired a man to work the farm for many years after that. Now she is retired but still lives all alone in that little farmhouse. It has been a dream of mine to visit her there and say thank you once again, but I have never had the opportunity.

"Maybe you and dad can go after I finish college."

"Perhaps, I have never talked about it with your father."

"How long did you stay with the Gagnons?" asked Rachel

"I stayed at their farm for about two weeks. They took a big chance by keeping me there. If the Germans had found out that they were hiding an escaped Jew, they would have been shot. I owe them my life.

"When I was healthy enough, they contacted the French Underground and told them of my presence there. The underground arranged for me to be smuggled on a French fishing boat to England. I had to hide in the compartment where they store the fish after catching them. The smell was so bad I vomited constantly. The French fishermen felt bad for me, but it was the best place to hide if we happened to get stopped by a Nazi patrol boat. Fortunately, we made it across the English Channel without being spotted.

"They anchored off a beach in England and rowed me ashore at night. The next morning I walked into a small English town. I remember that the people in the town were repulsed by my smell. Still, I somehow communicated to them my situation and they took me to the constable's office. I was allowed to clean myself and the constable provided me with a new dress from his wife. Within a few days I was put on a train to London and was met at the station by an official of the English government. I was taken to a building in London and they had someone there who spoke Polish. I told them my story, and also told them that I knew from my mother that we had distant relatives who lived in a place called Brooklyn in America. Within two weeks I was on an English merchant ship headed for New York. Two ships in our convoy were sunk by Nazi U boats. I was more frightened on that ship than I had been when I escaped the concentration camp. After everything I had been through, I did not want to die in the middle of the Atlantic Ocean on my way to America. I arrived here in the summer of 1941. All I had with me were the clothes on my back and your grandmother's necklace."

Mrs. Levy reached up and touched the necklace on her neck.

"That is grandma Emily's necklace?" asked Rachel, stunned.

"Yes, and someday when I am gone it will be yours. And hopefully someday you will give it to your daughter.

"Mom, I wish I could say something. I…I just don't

know…."

"Shhh, Rachel. It's okay. I have never told anyone this story. I have kept it inside me all these years. It feels good to finally let it out after carrying it so long."

"But mom, I……

"Rachel, when I met your father in early 1942, and he eventually asked me to marry him only a few months after we met, I thought I should tell him of my past and what had happened to me. As I said, he wouldn't let me. Perhaps even then I wasn't ready to talk about it, but I felt I owed it to him if I was going to be his wife. After what the German colonel had done to me at the camp, I wasn't even sure if I could bear another child. But your father just didn't want to know. He told me it made no difference and there was no reason for me to relive any pain. And so, to this day, you are now the only one who knows of all this."

Rachel leaned over and hugged her mother tightly. She started to cry.

"It's okay my girl," said Mrs. Levy "Don't you see now why I am the lucky one, and why this number on my arm is my lucky number? I have a loving husband, beautiful children, a wonderful home. Had I not gone through all that, I would have never come to America and met your father, and you and your brothers would not be here. I cannot even imagine what my life would be like without you and your brothers."

"Oh mom, how did you survive all that? How….."

"You just do, baby. I was determined to survive for my parents and my brother."

"My troubles seem so small and meaningless

compared to what you went through."

"But they are not, Rachel. There is too much hatred in this world. Too much pain. I have seen too much of it myself. To be in love, to love someone with your whole heart, that is such a good thing. If you love this boy Vincent, that is a good thing. Perhaps it will work out, and perhaps it won't. But if your heart tells you to love him, who am I, or even your father, to tell you who to love? But know my sweet girl if this does go on, you will face many difficulties."

"Are you going to tell Dad?"

"I told you I wouldn't. But perhaps when you feel the time is right, we should speak to him together."

Rachel hugged her mother again.

"I love you, mom."

"I love you."

Mrs. Levy kissed her daughter. She tucked in the blankets around Rachel as she settled down into bed. Rachel watched as her mother walked to the bedroom door and shut the light.

She listened to her mother's footsteps as she walked down the hall to her bedroom. When her mother's bedroom door shut, Rachel started to cry again. She cried until she drifted off to sleep.

CHAPTER EIGHT

By the time we got to Rachel's house the following Monday to start work, she had already left for school. I was torn. One part of me wanted to see her to apologize for being such a wise-ass and for getting mad. On the other hand, I thought about the fact that if I said something to her in her yard, and her father saw me, he would be upset with her for talking to me. This thought made me mad all over again.

On the way to work that morning, my father knew something was on my mind.

"You okay?" he asked as we sat at a red light.

"Yeah, fine.

"You don't look like everything is fine."

"I'm fine dad."

"You sure?"

"Yeah, I'm just tired."

"Well, seems to me something is bouncing around in your head.

"Dad, let's just drop it. I'm fine."

"Whatever you say."

The light changed and we turned onto Ocean Parkway. When we pulled up to Rachel's house my father took a moment to look over our work.

"Looks good," he said. "I figure we have two, maybe three more days. Hell, might as well take it to the end of the week. We can't go start another job until Monday anyway."

"Why? We've started plenty of jobs in the middle of the week."

"Well, I'm still the boss of this little operation, and I say we take it to Thursday or Friday. It ain't gonna cost Levy more money. The price I quoted him is the price he pays, doesn't matter how long the job takes. Capish?"

I understood that my father was doing this to give me more time to work things out with Rachel, one way or the other.

"Whatever," I said.

We started work at about eight, and around eight-thirty Mr. Levy came out of his front door on his way to work. I wanted to say something to him just to start a conversation. I wanted to see for myself what kind of guy he was. I certainly wasn't going to say anything to him about Rachel and me. Besides, one part of me was sure that the romance was going nowhere. My heart, however, was telling me something completely different.

I was at the end of the walkway. My father was by the stoop. My old man said good morning to Mr. Levy, and he replied in kind. As he walked toward me I scrambled in my head for something to say to him to start a short conversation. He walked by and just as he got to the gate I said, "Mr. Levy, can I ask you something?"

He stopped and turned toward me. "Excuse me?"

"I said, can I ask you something?"

"What is it?" he said impatiently

I had no idea what I wanted to ask him. Then it hit me. Rachel told me that at one time he was a big Brooklyn Dodger fan.

"Did you see Pistol Pete Reiser play in his prime?"

"Did I what?" he said, a bit confused.

"Did you see Pistol Pete play in his prime?"

"Yes I did."

I had no idea what to say next.

"What about Mr. Reiser?" he asked.

"Oh, I was just wondering. I never really saw him at his best. But people tell me he could have been one of the greatest players ever if he didn't keep hurting himself."

"I would say that's true. He could do it all, but he kept running into outfield fences chasing fly balls, and he ruined himself like that."

"I saw him at the end, when he was trying to make it back," I said.

"That was not the Pistol Pete I saw when he first came up. He was a superb ballplayer."

"I heard that. But he was a center fielder, right?"

"Yes, he was."

"Then, if he didn't get hurt, what would have happened when Duke Snider was ready to come up and play?"

"They probably would have moved Reiser to left. After all, even during those great years in the Fifties, the Dodgers never really had a good left fielder."

"That's true. They never really did. But then again, they had Sandy Amoros in left field in the seventh game of the '55 series, and if he wasn't out there to make that great catch against Yogi Berra, then the Yankees probably would have won that game and the World Series."

"That was quite a catch," Mr. Levy said.

Between 1941 and 1953 the Dodgers had played the Yankees five times in the World Series and lost every time. In fact, up until that point the Dodgers had never won a World Series in over seventy-five years of trying. And every time they lost to the Yankees, all us Dodger fans would say the same thing, "Wait 'til next year." Finally, in 1955 the Dodgers beat the Yankees in seven games to win their first and only World Championship while they were in Brooklyn. In the eighth inning of game seven of the '55 series, at Yankee Stadium, Dodger left fielder Sandy Amoros made an amazing catch of a drive by Yogi Berra that saved the game and the World Series for the Dodgers. The Yanks had two runners on base, and if Amoros had not made that catch, the Yankees would have tied the game at two, and then who knows what would have happened.

Mr. Levy had a kind of far off look in his eyes, as if he were remembering that wonderful year when we finally beat the Yankees. He didn't seem like a bad guy. He stood with me talking baseball like any other guy. My only thought was that this was the first time I had ever talked baseball with a guy in a yarmulke.

Suddenly his body stiffened, as if he had come back to his senses or something.

"I really don't have time for this," he said. "I have to

get to my office and you, young man, need to get to work as well. Please concentrate on your work and not on my daughter. Do you understand?"

I didn't say anything.

"I hope you understand," he said and then turned and headed up the sidewalk. I thought that was pretty rude. I got back on my knees to work on his walkway. I really didn't know what to think about the guy. Obviously he could be a nice guy, but he could be a jerk, too. Then again, I thought, that's probably true about all of us.

We left that day at around five and Rachel hadn't come home. I had all kinds of strange thoughts. She usually got home at about three or sometimes four. Where was she? Did she have another boyfriend already? Did she have a date with some guy her old man would approve of? Did she meet some nice Jewish boy at school? I couldn't keep these thoughts from bouncing around in my head. It made my stomach hurt. Next time I saw her I'd probably have to use all the self control I had not to start asking her a million questions about where she was. But then I thought, what business is it of mine? As far as I was concerned, unless she told her father the truth, I didn't know if I could continue seeing her. Of course in my heart I knew I was lying to myself. I knew in my heart that I would do anything to see her again. I would do anything to kiss her and hold her again. Even sneaking around so her old man didn't find out. I tried to be logical about it and tell myself that I'd be a fool to do that, but my heart just wouldn't listen. But how was I going to tell her this? I couldn't talk to her at her house in case her father saw us. I couldn't call her on the phone. I could just imagine what it would be like for her if her father caught her on the phone talking to me. I had no idea what I wanted to do. All I knew was that I had to talk to her.

I didn't see Rachel on Tuesday or Wednesday. My father had decided that we would finish up on Friday, so at least I had two more days. After that we had to move on to a job in Flatbush, which was miles away from Rachel's house.

On Thursday afternoon at around three, I saw Rachel coming down the sidewalk toward her house. I had made up my mind to stop her. At that point I didn't care if her father saw us. He usually got home at around 2:30 or three in the afternoon, so he was there most of the time when Rachel came home from school. I didn't care. I had been living with a knot in my stomach all week, and I had to know one way or the other what was going on.

As Rachel turned into her yard I looked up at her. She didn't look down at me. As she passed me she dropped a folded up piece of paper in front of me.

"Hey Rachel," I said, but she kept right on going into her front door. I picked up the piece of paper and read it.

Vincent,

Call me at two o'clock tomorrow at AN-5-3476. It's a payphone at school. It's between my classes and I can talk, Rachel

I took my lunch break at about a quarter to two on Friday. I had to walk four blocks to find the nearest payphone. I dropped a dime, dialed the number and it rang once before it was answered.

"Hello," a voice said.

"Can I speak to Rachel, please."

"This is me, Vincent."

"Oh, sorry, I just never heard your voice on the phone before."

"Who else was going to answer?"

"What? Are you the wise-ass now?"

"No, I could never be in your class."

"Yeah, well, I wanted to apologize about that."

"No need to. I understand that you were upset."

"Listen, Rachel, I.......

"Vincent," she interrupted, "we have to talk about this. I've been so upset for the last five days. It's like I always have this empty feeling in my stomach."

"Yeah," I said, "I know the feeling."

"We need to meet."

"I know, Rachel, but where? I'm sick of benches and busses."

"I'll come over to your neighborhood tomorrow."

"You what?"

"I said, I'll come over to your neighborhood."

"Why?"

"Because it's the best place. There's no way my father will see us. Plus, there isn't going to be anybody my father knows who'll see us."

"You sure you want to come and be with us lowlife Italians?"

"Vincent, do you have to be such a smart aleck?"

"I'm sorry, I shouldn't have said that."

"Where should we meet?" she asked.

"Well, what time can you come over?"

"After temple, probably at about twelve or so."

"Okay, there's this little Italian café on the corner of Coney Island Avenue and Avenue Z. It's called Stramiello's."

"What?"

"Stramiello's. It's like a coffee shop, café kind of place. It's got cakes and stuff in the window. They have tables inside. We can sit and talk."

"I'm assuming it's not a kosher place."

"No, definitely not. I think Mrs. Stramiello is Sicilian."

There was a moment of silence.

"Rachel, listen," I said. "I'm really sorry about what I said. I was just getting mad and then I get to be a wise-ass sometimes and...."

"It's okay Vincent. I understand."

"You do?"

"Of course I do. I guess I would be mad, too, if it were the other way around."

"It's just that I....."

"Vincent, let's talk about it tomorrow, okay?"

"Okay."

"See you at around twelve."

"You want me to order something for us to eat?"

"I don't think I can eat anything there."

"It's good food."

"It's not that, it's....never mind, I'll explain

tomorrow."

"Okay."

"So twelve?"

"Yeah."

"I'll see you then."

"Rachel, you know, I love you."

It just came out of my mouth. I had no control.

"I have to go, Vincent. I have a class."

"Okay, see you tomorrow."

"Good-by Vincent."

"Yeah, so long."

And then she hung up the phone.

I didn't know if I felt better or worse. It was wonderful to hear her voice. It was wonderful to know I was going to see her again. But I didn't like the way she ended the conversation. Why didn't she tell me she loved me? I told her. Maybe she had just come to the conclusion that there was no way we could stay together and she wanted to tell me in person. I had already made up my mind that I was going to do whatever it took to make it work between us. Maybe I was too late. Maybe I should have listened to her the first time. The only conclusion I could come to was that being this much in love was the single-most confusing thing I had ever experienced.

CHAPTER NINE

When I got to Stramiello's at eleven-thirty on Saturday morning my friends, Mole and Eyeballs, were sitting at a table eating Italian pastries and drinking coffee. Stramiello's was a small place, with a kitchen in the back, a counter in front filled with bread and Italian pastries, and about twelve tables on the floor. Mrs. Stramiello, who ran the place since her husband died, was known throughout the neighborhood for giving you more food than you could possibly eat. If you ordered a sandwich and she didn't think it was enough to fill you up, she'd give you another sandwich free of charge. She just couldn't get over her Italian mother's instinct to feed you until you were full. We all knew this and often hung out there. We'd order a pastry or a sandwich, but as long as we sat there Mrs. Stramiello kept the food coming.

Mrs. Stramiello was in her sixties with short white hair. She was about five feet tall and was built kind of like a fire hydrant. She had come over from Sicily as a girl of ten and never lost her heavy Italian accent. We all learned to understand her quite well. When I walked into the café she was standing by Mole and Eyeball's table urging them to eat more.

"You sure you no wanna no more?" she said. "You looka like you maybe still hungry."

"Please, Mrs. S.," said Mole, "we're stuffed."

"Maybe I'll have another cannoli," said Eyeballs. He was a real skinny guy, but he could eat enormous amounts of food. We were constantly amazed at the amount of macaroni he could consume at one sitting and never gain a pound.

"I getta you more, Edward, you too Anthony," she said. She always called us by our real names, as opposed to the nicknames we all had. She walked to the counter to get them more pastries and that's when Mole saw me standing by the door.

"Yo, Bricks," he said

"Hey Mole, hey Eyeballs," I said.

I walked to their table and sat down. I hadn't expected to see them there and I was hoping they would leave before Rachel arrived. Stramiello's was usually pretty empty on a Saturday afternoon. During the week the cafe was packed in the morning and afternoon for breakfast and lunch, and Sunday there was always a big crowd after church, but Saturdays were usually slow.

"What are you up to?" Mole asked as I sat.

"Nothing, just wanted to get some espresso and a cannoli."

Mrs. Stramiello came back to the table with a tray of pastry and two more cups of cappuccino for Mole and Eyeballs.

"Vincenzo," she said to me, "you wanna eat sometin'?"

"No Mrs. S., I'll wait a bit."

"No, you eat. Why you come inna here if you no

eat?"

"Yeah," said Mole, "why you come inna here if you no eat?"

"I'm fine," I said, "I'll get something a little later."

"I getta you the coffee, you want?"

"Yeah, that would be great, Mrs. S., espresso, thanks."

She waddled off and Mole looked at me suspiciously.

"What's up with you?" he asked.

"Nothing."

"Nothing? You come in here and you don't want anything to eat?"

"Not right now."

"Then when?" said Eyeballs.

"What's with you guys?" I said. "You have to know everything?"

"Absolutely," said Mole.

I had no choice. "Look, you guys, I'm meeting a girl here in a little while and….."

"What girl?" asked Eyeballs.

"It's got to be that Jewish girl," Mole said. "You know, the one he was meeting when me and you had to walk up and down Ocean Parkway with him to see how fast he could go five blocks when he had to meet her on his lunch break."

"Yeah, that girl," I said.

"When is she getting here?" asked Eyeballs

"What does that matter?" I said. "You guys won't be here anyway."

"Oh, I don't think so, Bricks," Mole said. "Do you

think there's any way we're gonna possibly leave until we see what this girl looks like? You should know better than that."

"You know, Mole, you're a real pain in the ass sometimes," I said.

"I pride myself on that fact."

"Do me a favor, will you?" I said. "Just don't be assholes about it, okay?"

"Come on, Bricks," said Eyeballs, "when were we ever assholes?"

"I'd tell you," I said, "but there ain't enough time."

"Now you're hurting our feelings," said Mole.

"Just don't be assholes," I said.

Mrs. Stramiello brought me my coffee, and I told her I would be moving to a table near the back because I was meeting somebody in about twenty minutes.

"Who you meet?" she asked.

"A girl," said Mole

"Yeah, his new girlfriend," added Eyeballs.

"What?" said Mrs. Stramiello. "You no see dat Rosemarie girl no more."

"No, Mrs. S. I haven't seen her for a long time."

"When-a you new girlfriend get here, I make-a you something nice for da lunch."

"You don't have to do that Mrs. S.," I said. "I don't know if we're gonna eat."

"How you no eat?"

"Yeah," said Eyeballs, "how you no eat?"

"We'll see," I said.

"I make-a you sometin' just inna case."

"That's fine Mrs. S.," I said.

Mrs. Stramiello walked away and Mole watched her go. He turned back toward me.

"You know, Bricks, if you didn't want anybody to know about this, coming here wasn't the brightest idea you ever had. Not that you've had many bright ideas in your life. You know Mrs. S. talks to everybody who comes in here. I'd say within a day of you being here with.......What's her name?"

"Rachel."

"Within a day of you being here with Rachel, the whole neighborhood is gonna know about this."

"I don't care."

"Good," said Eyeballs, "as long as you don't care."

We sat and talked for another fifteen minutes or so, then I moved to a table toward the back of the café.

A few minutes later Rachel appeared at the doorway. She was wearing a green print dress and a white shirt and her hair was down. She looked beautiful. I glanced at my friends who were trying to be discreet, which was something they weren't very good it. They both stared at her. I jumped up from the table and went to the door.

"Hey Rachel," I said.

"Hi Vincent."

I wanted to kiss her, but I wasn't sure what to do. I decided it was probably not a good idea at that moment.

"Come on," I said, "let's go sit down."

I led her to the table in the back.

"It smells wonderful in here," she said as we sat.

"Yeah, that's all the pastries and the coffee

brewing."

As soon as we sat down, Mrs. Stramiello came rushing over to the table with an antipasto tray.

"Here," she said, "you mangia on this for now, I bring-a you more if you want."

"Thanks Mrs. S.," I said.

"Sure, sure, you tell-a me iffa you want more, Capish?"

"Capish," I said, and Mrs. S. headed back to the kitchen.

"We didn't even order anything," Rachel said.

"I know, Mrs. Stramiello thinks it's her sacred mission in life to feed everybody she possibly can."

Rachel looked at the antipasto tray.

"My God, this smells so good."

"Do you know what any of this stuff is?"

"Actually, no."

I pointed out the roasted peppers, mozzarella, dried sausage, artichoke hearts, provolone and proscuito.

"I don't think I've ever even seen this kind of food, let alone eat it. I don't think there's anything on that tray I'm allowed to eat," Rachel said.

"We eat food like this everyday."

Mrs. Stramiello came over to the table again with a basket of fresh Italian bread.

"Grazie," I said.

She looked at Rachel. "You mangia," she said to her. "You gotta no meat on you bones. The boys, they like-a little meat on da bones."

Rachel looked at her and smiled but said nothing.

"Yes, you mangia." said Mrs. S. She walked away

and Rachel looked at me with a smile.

"What exactly did she just tell me?" she asked.

"She wants you to eat because you look too skinny. You know, mangia. It means eat."

"I really can't eat any of it because it's not kosher."

"What exactly does this kosher thing mean?" I asked. "I always heard the word, but I'm not sure exactly what it means. I know that at Easter time, when you guys have Passover, they sell all this special kosher food at the grocery store. "

"Well, the food has to be blessed by a rabbi. And there are a lot of other rules, too. We're not supposed to eat pork, and we're not supposed to eat meat and dairy products at the same time. Things like that. There's a whole bunch of rules. Will Mrs....ah?"

"Just call her Mrs. S."

"Will she be upset if I don't eat anything?"

"Probably. Don't worry, I'll eat some stuff."

From across the café I heard Mole clear his throat very loudly. I looked over at him and then back at Rachel.

"And those two peppers over there at the other table are friends of mine. They're trying to act like they're just here hanging around, but they're actually watching every move we make. They wanted to see what you looked like."

Rachel looked at Mole and Eyeballs, and both of them smiled and waved.

"Come here, you idiots," I said.

They came over and stood by our table.

"Rachel," I said, "this is my friend Mole Martinelli

and my friend Eyeballs Casola. Guys, this is Rachel Levy"

"Very nice to meet you," Rachel said.

"Nice to meet you," they said together.

"They were just leaving," I said.

"Actually, we weren't," Mole said to me. "Rachel doesn't even know our real names." He turned toward her. "Rachel, I'm Anthony Francis Martinelli, known to all as 'Mole.' That's because I used to have a mole on my chin when I was a kid, but when we were six, Bricks here cut it off with a scissors, for which I will always be grateful."

"Is that true, Vincent?" asked Rachel in amazement.

"Well....kind of." I said.

"It's absolutely true," said Mole, then he turned to Eyeballs. "And this here is the legendary Edward Angelo Vito Luigi Francesco Casola. Did I forget any of your many names, Eyeballs?"

"Not a one."

"Good," Mole continued. "We call him Eyeballs because without those very thick glasses you see on his face, ol' Eyeballs can't see two feet in front of him. Isn't that right, Eyeballs?"

"Every word of it. These glasses are my eyeballs."

"And we are both very happy to meet you, Rachel," Mole finished with a flourish. He then bent at the waist, picked up Rachel's left hand and kissed it.

Rachel smiled.

"Awright, that's it," I said. "Enough with the Rudolph Valentino crap. Say good-by now."

Mole totally ignored me.

"Hey Rachel," he said, "did you know that when Bricks here was supposed to meet you on the bench at Avenue Z, he took me and Eyeballs up to Ocean Parkway and had us timing him walking from your house to the bench and back to see how long it took?"

Rachel smiled again. "Yes, I know about that. Vincent actually told me about it."

"Vincent? Vincent?" said Eyeballs, turning toward Mole. "Do we know anybody named Vincent? We know a Bricks. We know a Vinny. But Vincent? I don't think so."

Rachel giggled a little. "You guys are funny," she said.

"Yeah," I said, "a regular Abbott and Costello. And they were on their way out."

"Yeah, we have to go," said Mole. "It was very nice to meet you Rachel."

"It was nice meeting you."

Mole turned to Eyeballs. "Come on Costello, let's go."

Mole grabbed Eyeballs by the shirt and pulled him toward the door, while Eyeballs, doing his best Lou Costello imitation, kept repeating "Hey Abbott!"

All I could do was shake my head.

"Your friends are funny," Rachel said.

"We've known each other since we were babies. They're really good guys, and good friends, besides being jerks."

"They weren't jerks."

"You don't know them as well as I do."

Mrs. Stramiello came over to our table again.

"How come you no eat?"

"We'll eat, Mrs. S., don't worry," I said.

"Look," she said, "I no allowed to sell you da wine here. But I gotta little bottle thatsa mine in back. I make it myself. You want?"

"Not a whole bottle," I said.

"Then I bringa da glasses."

Before I could say anything she was off and returned a moment later with two small glasses of wine. They weren't actually glasses. They were jelly jars.

"Anybody ask-a, you say its da grape juice. Capish?"

"Okay," I said, and she walked away.

"My God, I can't get over how good this smells," Rachel said, looking at the antipasto platter.

"Well, try some."

"I can't, Vincent, it's not kosher."

"So what's gonna happen? If you have some God's gonna strike you dead or something?"

"No."

"Then here, try a little bit, just a little."

I took a hunk of fresh Italian bread, dipped it in the olive oil at the bottom of the platter, then put a piece of roasted pepper on it and a small piece of mozzarella.

"Just try this," I said.

"I really shouldn't."

"Yes, you really should. It's really good."

"I'm sure it's good. I'm just not supposed to."

"Just try it. I'm sure you won't be doomed forever to hell for eating a little antipasto. Besides, Mrs. S.

might get upset if you don't. I don't know all that much about heaven and hell, but I do know you don't want to get Mrs. S. pissed off."

Rachel exhaled. "Okay, just this once."

I handed her the piece of bread and she slowly put it in her mouth and began to chew. A look of absolute pleasure came to her face. She closed her eyes and chewed slowly.

"Oh my God," she said.

"What?"

"Oh my God."

"What, what?"

"That is the best thing I have ever tasted in my life," she said.

"Rachel, that ain't nothing. That's just what we eat before dinner."

"This is not like a meal or anything?"

"Not even close. Here, try this."

I picked up a bigger piece of bread and put a piece of roasted pepper on it, a piece of provolone and a small piece of sweet dried sausage.

"Does that meat have pork in it?" she asked.

"I think so. Why?

"I can't have any kind of pork at all."

"Really."

"None, of any kind."

"Why?"

"That's just the rules."

"Not nothing? Not bacon, or ham, or pork roast, or nothing?"

"Nothing."

"Wow, that's tough."

"We can't eat anything that came from a pig."

"Okay, we'll get rid of the sausage just in case." I took the piece of sausage off the bread and replaced it with a piece of mozzarella. I handed her the bread. "After you chew it a little, take a small sip of wine. Can you drink wine?"

"Well, on some holidays, like Passover, we have some sweet wine."

"Try it.

She did.

"Oh my God. This is amazing."

"I know."

In the next fifteen minutes we wiped out the entire platter of antipasto. Rachel wouldn't touch the sausage or the proscuito, but she ate everything else. This made Mrs. Stramiello very, very happy. She came over to our table to get our empty tray.

"You wanna more?" she asked.

"No, please Mrs. S., we're stuffed," I said.

"That was very good, thank you," Rachel said.

"I'm glad you like. You sure you no wanna no more?"

"No thank you," said Rachel.

"I bring-a da cappuccino and cannoli."

Before we could refuse her offer, Mrs. Stramiello was off again and came back a minute later with the cappuccino and a cannoli for each of us.

"What's this?" Rachel asked, looking at the cannoli in front of her.

"Don't tell me you never even saw a cannoli?"

"Where would I have seen one?"

"I guess nowhere. Try it, but you have to do the same thing like we did with the wine. Take a bite of the cannoli, then take a sip of the cappuccino. Careful, the cappuccino is hot."

She did as I told her and one more time she got that look of absolute pleasure on her face.

"I told you it was good," I said.

"You eat like this all the time?"

"Everyday."

"My God, you should weigh 300 pounds."

"Not really, everything is kind of balanced."

"Well, if there's one thing I learned today, it's that kosher food really kind of stinks, especially compared to this."

"I'm sure there's good kosher food."

"Not much."

"Well you know, some people eat to live, we Italians live to eat."

She smiled and we looked into each other's eyes. Rachel had met Mole and Eyeballs, we had eaten a big tray of antipasto, and we hadn't even spoken about the subject that brought us there in the first place. Us.

"Vincent, we need to...."

"No Rachel, listen to me. I was wrong to say some of the things I said about your father and the whole situation. I guess I understand why it would be so hard for you."

"Do your parents know?"

"Well, my father kind of knows, but not my mother."

"What's she going to say?"

"I'm not sure. She ain't gonna be happy at first, I know that. But I'm gonna talk to her tonight after dinner. Besides, people been coming in and out of here all morning, and I guarantee by this afternoon everybody in the neighborhood's gonna know I was in here with a girl nobody has ever seen before. I figure I better tell my mom before she hears it through the neighborhood grapevine."

"I still can't say anything to my father, not yet," she said softly. "And if because of that you can't..."

"But I can."

"Can what?"

"I can deal with it. I have to. For now. Look, not talking to you for five days, not seeing you, the whole time I had a knot in my stomach. We'll just do what we have to do until you think the time is right to tell your old man. All I know is that I don't want to feel like I felt all last week."

"Neither do I."

"I mean, we can figure it out. I know that after I talk to my parents, I'm sure you can come to my house every once and a while. And Brooklyn is a big place. I'm sure we can find places to go."

"I know we can."

"I know I can't call your house, but you can call mine and then we can figure out when we're gonna see each other. It'll work. For a while anyway."

"I think it's worth it," said Rachel. "I know it is. I had a long talk with my mother a few nights ago. She knows about us."

"What?"

"She knows about us."

"Did you tell her?"

"No, but she said she knew just by looking at me that I was in love, and she knew it had to be you. She called you that Italian boy."

"Oh man."

"It's okay, she promised she wouldn't say anything to my father until I was ready. She also told me something else."

"What?"

"She finally told me the story of her time in the concentration camp, and how she escaped."

"I thought she didn't want to talk about that."

"That's what she always told me, but I guess she was ready for me to hear it. I've been asking her about it for so many years. She's never even told my father about it. I am the only one she has ever told."

"Was it bad?"

"I can't even describe the horrors she went through. She made me promise I would not tell anyone else. But there is one thing."

"What's that?"

"She told me of a French couple named the Gagnons who took her in when she reached France after escaping the camp, and they nursed her back to health at their farm. She said she owes them her life and it's always been her dream to visit them and say thank you again. The husband died right after the war, but the wife still lives on the farm. Her dream is now my dream. I'd like to be able to send her there someday."

"And you will, Rachel," I said.

"It better be soon. Mrs. Gagnon has to be very old now."

I leaned over the table and kissed Rachel softly on the lips. I felt that electricity shoot through my body again. It was an amazing feeling. It happened every time I touched her or kissed her or even just saw her walking towards me.

Mrs. Stramiello came over to the table.

"You eat more?" she asked.

"Not a thing, Mrs. S.," I said.

"I'd like something," said Rachel, obviously much to my surprise. "I'd like another cannoli, please."

"Good, thatsa good. You such a pretty girl, but you needa some meat on da bones. Da boys, they like-a some meat on da bones."

Mrs. Stramiello started to walk to the counter, then stopped and turned back to us. "Vincenzo, kiss the pretty girl again, then-a I come back with the cannoli."

I leaned over the table and kissed Rachel again. At that moment in time I was completely and absolutely content and happy with the world and my life. I noticed out of the corner of my eye that Mole and Eyeballs had returned and were standing in the doorway watching us. I sat back in my chair.

I turned to the door. "Hey peppers, what are you looking at?"

Eyeballs looked down, a bit embarrassed. Mole, who I think was never embarrassed in his life, smiled.

"Look," Rachel said, "Abbott and Costello have

returned."

"Well, you know, we have to watch out for our boy Bricks," said Mole.

"Don't worry about that," said Rachel. "I'll take care of him."

It was late September of 1962. I was as happy as I had ever been in my life.

A little over a year later, my world came crashing down around me.

CHAPTER TEN

On the samc Saturday I met with Rachel at Stamiello's, I wanted to talk to my parents about her but I chickened out. I had planned to tell them after dinner, but my kid sister Marie had a fever and they were focused on her, so I let it slide until Sunday.

We always ate early on Sunday, about three o'clock, and so after we finished our macaroni I told my parents I needed to talk to them. My mother wanted to clean the kitchen first. In an Italian home, the kitchen is the most important room in the house. You ate in the kitchen, did your homework on the kitchen table, had arguments in the kitchen, and had serious talks in the kitchen.

I sat at the table and watched my mother clean. She was meticulous. You could eat off the floor in our house. My mom was tall for a woman, about five-foot-eight, and thin. It ran in her family. Her older brother, my late Uncle Nick, was about six-foot-five. My mother had light brown hair and much finer and sharper facial features than my dad. I definitely got my height and my facial features from my mother's side of the family.

Although my mother's parents were Sicilian and had dark skin, mom was quite fair. Before she married my father she was a dressmaker in the garment district in Manhattan. She was a genius with a needle and thread or a sewing machine. She had made her own wedding dress, which was absolutely beautiful, and she was very proud of the fact that after twenty-two years of marriage, her wedding dress still fit perfectly. She still made her own dresses for special occasions.

After mom finished cleaning the kitchen she wiped her hands with a dishtowel and sat down at the table.

"Can dad come in, too," I said.

"What's wrong, Vincent?"

"Nothing's wrong ma, I just want to talk to both of you."

She called for my father who walked in and sat at his usual spot at the head of the table.

"What's going on?" he said.

I took a deep breath. "I wanted to tell you guys something, that's all."

"Is everything okay?" my mother asked.

"Yeah, everything is fine," I said.

My father looked at me and folded his hands. He always did that when he got serious.

"I have a feeling this is about the job we just finished on Ocean Parkway, isn't it?" he said.

"What about it?" asked Mom.

"It's nothing about the job," said my father, "but it has to do with it."

"Will one of you explain to me what you're talking about?" my mother asked.

"Ma," I said, "I am seeing a new girl."

"That's wonderful, hon. Is she from around here?"

"Well, yeah, she's from around here, but not exactly

from around here."

"What does that mean?"

"Well, she lives within a few blocks of here, but she's not exactly from this neighborhood."

"So, where exactly is she from?"

"Ocean Parkway."

My mother stared at me for a moment. I think at first she wasn't really sure what I meant. Then, from the look on her face, I knew it had suddenly dawned on her.

"What part of Ocean Parkway?" she asked.

"The Jewish part," I said.

"The Jewish part?" she said.

"Yes."

"Vincent, tell your mother what you have to tell her," said my father. "I already have a good idea of what's going on with you."

"The Jewish part," my mother said softly to herself.

"Yeah, ma, the Jewish part. I'm seeing a girl named Rachel Levy and she's Jewish."

"How did that happen?" she said.

"I met her on the job we just finished. She's in college." I thought I'd add that, as it might impress my mother.

She seemed a bit stunned by the whole thing, as if she couldn't actually comprehend what I had just told her.

"What exactly are you saying, Vincent?" she asked.

"I'm saying that I am seeing a Jewish girl from Ocean Parkway, and I wanted you and dad to know."

My mother turned to my father.

"Angelo, did you know about this?"

"Well, I had an idea."

She turned back to me.

"Vincent, do you really think that's a good idea?"

"I don't see what's wrong with it, ma."

"There's a lot of things wrong with it. You're a Catholic boy. Do you realize how different that is from being Jewish?"

"Yeah, I know."

"Is she, ah, just what you would call a normal Jew, or is she very religious?" she asked.

"She's an Orthodox Jew."

"Oh my God, Vincent."

"What's the big deal, ma?"

"Vincent, I don't know a lot about it. But I do know that the Orthodox Jews are very, very religious."

"Is that a bad thing, ma?"

"I didn't say it was a bad thing. But if it's totally opposite of what you believe, then it's a very big problem."

"Ma, it's totally opposite of what you believe, but maybe not what I believe."

"What exactly does that mean?" she said.

"It means that, yeah, I'm Catholic, but I'm maybe not as, you know, serious as you about it."

"It has nothing to do with how serious you are about being Catholic. It's the differences in the way we see things and the way we live. Do you understand that?"

I didn't answer.

"Vincent, how serious are you about this girl?"

asked my father.

"Pretty serious, dad."

"How long have you known her?" asked my mother.

"About three weeks."

"How can you possibly be serious about her after only three weeks?"

"I don't know, ma, but I am. I never felt like this before."

"What do her parents think about it?"

I was hoping she wouldn't ask me that.

"I don't know," I said, wanting to avoid the subject entirely.

"What, she never said anything about her parents to you?" my mother asked.

My father shifted in his chair. He knew, from the talk he had had with Mr. Levy, that Mr. Levy didn't even want me talking to Rachel let alone dating her. My father gave me a look that told me I had better just come clean.

"Her father doesn't even know we're seeing each other," I said.

"And why is that?" my mother said.

"Because her father only wants her to date Jewish guys."

"Well, sounds to me like he understands what I'm trying to tell you, and he doesn't want to see his daughter hurt or have her heart broken."

"I'm not going to break her heart."

"Maybe you don't want to, but it's going to happen just because of the differences."

"What does that mean?"

"It means that the differences between Catholics and Jews are just too basic for it to go smoothly between you two."

"Ma," I said, "do you just not like Jewish people?"

"Vincent, you know better than that. I don't not like anybody for their religion or anything like that. But there are differences between what people believe, and sometimes those differences are so big you can't overcome them."

"I don't believe that," I said.

"You don't believe that because you really like this girl. I understand that. But you're not old enough yet to understand what could happen if you got married and all the complications that would cause."

"Who said anything about getting married, ma?"

"I know you didn't. But let's just say this continued, and you fell in love with her and wanted to get married."

"I do love her."

"Fine. So let's say the day comes that you want to marry her. Where do you get married, a church or a synagogue? Do you think her parents will let her get married in any place but a synagogue? You're Catholic, you can't get married in a synagogue. And what about kids? Are they Jewish or Catholic? What do you teach them? They'd probably have to be Jewish because of the mother. And what about food?"

"Food?" I said.

"Don't the really religious Jews have rules about what they can eat?"

"Yeah," I said, "the food has to be kosher, and they can't eat pork, or something like that."

"So even something as simple as dinner is a problem. She can't make you meatballs because they have pork in them. My God, most of the food you love to eat wouldn't be allowed. Are you going to have a rabbi come into your house and bless all the macaroni?"

"Mom, I can't believe we're even talking about this. I didn't say I was gonna marry the girl. I mean, I love her, but I only know her three weeks."

"Vincent, don't you understand what I'm saying? What's the point of going on with it if there is no future because of the differences?"

"Felicia, slow down here," said my father. "Vincent isn't getting married any time soon. He's going to school for two years starting next September. Why don't we all just be patient and see what happens."

"Angelo, you're missing my point. What do you mean see what happens? My point is, if this thing goes on I don't see it leading to anything but problems and heartache."

"How can you know that, ma?"

"I just do."

We sat in silence for a moment.

"I want to be able to have her over the house," I said.

"Vincent, you know that everybody is welcome in our house," my mother said. "I just don't want to see you get hurt."

"Mom, I'm gonna keep seeing Rachel no matter

what. I love her and that's what my heart tells me. Didn't you always tell me that the best decisions you make in life are the ones made with your heart?"

"Yes I did. But you also need common sense."

"So can I bring her here?"

"Of course you can," my mother said. "You know that. I just don't think the whole relationship is a good idea for a lot of reasons."

"Ma, if that's true, then I'm just gonna have to find out for myself."

"But you can't go over her house, right?" said my mother.

"No."

"And why not?"

"Because like I told you, right now her father can't even know I'm seeing her."

"What about her mother?"

"She knows, but she promised she wouldn't say anything to the old man until Rachel was ready to tell him."

"Doesn't that tell you something?" my mother asked.

"What?"

"Please, Vincent, think about it. Her father doesn't want you anywhere near this girl. Don't you see what kind of problems that can cause in the future?"

"Ma, I'm just gonna see what happens. That's all I can do."

"Honey, I just want what's best for you. If you love this girl than you know she's welcome in our home. You know that. But all I can see in the future is problems and difficulties and hurt, and you can understand why I want to protect you from that."

"I know, ma. But this is how I feel right now."

"Okay Vincent, it's your decision. I can't tell you what to do or who to fall in love with. I just don't think any good can come from this."

"I don't know, ma. But I know I just can't walk away from it. I've never felt like this about any girl before. I know it's only been a short time, but that really doesn't matter. It's what I feel that matters."

My mother reached out and put her hand over mine. "Vincent, you do what you have to do. You're old enough to make your own decisions, even if I don't agree with you. I guess there are some things you just have to find out for yourself."

The next year flew by. Rachel and I met whenever and wherever we could. Sometimes I'd take a day off from work and we'd meet at her school. During the spring and summer we spent a lot of time at the Coney Island amusement park. It was easy to get lost in the crowd there. She came over to my house at least one night a week. We'd sit on the couch in the parlor and just talk, or we'd go for a walk in the neighborhood. It turned out my mother really liked Rachel. She was such a sweet girl that my mother couldn't help but see the goodness in her. My mom never lost her reservations and worries about the difficulties we would face in the future, but like me, she was taking it a day at time.

Each time Rachel and I saw each other our love grew stronger. Sometimes we couldn't see each other for three or four days in a row and it was torture. The hours just dragged on until we could meet again. We went to a lot of movies, too. Mostly we sat way in the back of the theater and kissed for two hours. Just being in each other's company was enough. There was always such a wonderful feeling of love, contentment and warmth.

During the entire year, Rachel's father never gave her any indication that he knew we were seeing each other. Sometimes she thought that her father had his suspicions, but he never said anything and Rachel wasn't going to bring it up herself, not yet anyway. Often I would press her about finally telling her father, but I knew from her reaction that she wasn't ready. I didn't pursue it any further because I didn't want our time together to be spent arguing. I didn't want to waste one minute of this precious time.

In July of 1963, Rachel and I actually started talking about getting married. She had graduated school in June and was working full time for her father. I was going to start school in September. We figured out how she could continue to work and save money while I finished school. We talked about the difficulties we would face, but we both honestly felt everything could be overcome. The only major hurdle would be when and how we told her father about us. That always hung over our heads like a sword.

The other thing that hung over our heads like a sword was the trip Rachel was making to Israel in

September. She would be gone for a little over three weeks and I just didn't want her to go. She told me she had to go. She had no choice. Everyone in her family had been there and it was her turn now that she had graduated college. I think a part of her really didn't want to go, but she was resigned to the fact that she had no choice in the matter. I insisted that she did have a choice. I told her to just tell her father she wasn't going. That she was a grown woman and could make her own decisions. "No," she'd say, "It's going to be tough enough when I tell him about us and our plans. If I tell him that I don't want to go to Israel, the whole thing between us will be impossible."

She had decided she would tell her father about us after she got back from Israel. She felt that at that point she would have met all her obligations to her father, and the time would be right. I guess maybe she was right, but I still didn't want her to go away.

In late August we went to Coney Island to have a dinner picnic on the beach. By this time Rachel was no longer "strictly kosher" in what she ate. She still wouldn't touch pork, but just about everything else was fine. Obviously she ate only kosher food at home, but when we were out she ate pizza, Chinese food and Italian food. It was like a whole new world opened up to her. I told her that my mother would teach her how to cook Italian food, because that food was part of my soul.

I made some chicken cutlet sandwiches for our picnic and got a bottle of good red wine from my father's liquor cabinet. September was coming up quickly and I wanted this night to be special. I had spent three days looking in jewelry stores to buy Rachel a special gift - something she could wear while she was in Israel, to always remind her of our love. I found a beautiful diamond and emerald bracelet. I couldn't wait to give it to her.

We got to the beach around six o'clock. It had emptied out by that time. The boardwalk was full of people and the amusement park was packed, but the beach was practically deserted. We went far past where the boardwalk ended, and picked a spot in front of some tall apartment buildings that overlooked the Atlantic Ocean. We put the blanket down and ate, and drank my father's bottle of wine. We didn't talk much, but we didn't have to. There was total contentment and joy in just being together on a beautiful August night.

The summer was ending soon and I would start college while Rachel went off on her adventure in Israel. So there was some sadness, too, that night.

I sat with my arm around her as we looked out on the dark water. "What day do you leave again?" I asked. "I keep forgetting because I just don't want to think about you going away."

"I leave on September 21st at five o'clock in the evening."

"Guess I won't be coming to the airport to see you off?"

"We already talked about that, Vincent. We'll meet that morning at Stramiello's to say our good-byes."

"With Italians we never say good-bye, that's too

final. We say so long which means until next time."

"We'll say our so longs that morning."

"Rachel, I got something for you. Something I want you to always keep with you when you're away."

"You didn't have to do that Vincent. You'll be in my heart always."

"Yes, I had to do it."

I reached into the picnic basket and pulled out the small box that held the diamond and emerald bracelet and handed it to her.

She looked into my eyes, then kissed me.

"Open it, baby," I said.

She slowly took the top off the small box and her mouth dropped open in amazement.

"Oh my God, Vincent! This is the most beautiful thing I have ever seen. Why did you do this?"

"Because I love you, and I want you to have that on your wrist all the time. This way you can just look down at it and know what you mean to me."

She took it out of the box and handed it to me.

"Put in on me."

I did. It sparkled on her slender wrist.

"You know, I can't wear this at home because my father will want to know where I got it," she said

"I know."

"But as soon as I get on the plane, I'll put it on and never take it off until I see you again when I get back."

"Good, this way when some dark, handsome Israeli guy is trying to charm you, all you have to do is look at your wrist."

"You know that could never happen."

"Well, you know, you're in a foreign, exotic land, there's some guy with an accent, you're beautiful, you know."

"Are you really worried about that?"

"I think about it. Actually I think about it a lot."

"That could never happen."

"Well, I have to trust you. It's not like I have a choice in the matter. If I had a choice, you wouldn't be going in the first place."

"Please Vincent, let's not go over that again. Don't ruin the night."

"I know, I know. It's just that the thought of not seeing you for three weeks is killing me."

"It's killing me, too. It'll go by quick."

"Not quick enough."

"You'll finally be in school, and you'll be very busy. You'll see how quick the time goes by."

"Like I said, not quick enough."

"And what about you?"

"What about me?"

"You're going to be in school with all these girls around. You're a tall, handsome guy. Don't you think the girls are going to be after you?"

"They don't have a shot."

I kissed her. We wrapped our arms around each other and fell back on the blanket.

We made love for the first time on a blanket on the beach that night at Coney Island. She was a virgin. I wasn't, but I felt like one.

CHAPTER ELEVEN

School started for me on September 7th. I planned to work with my father right up until the day before I began classes. Depending on the size of the job, my father would sometimes hire workers to help us. He told me that with me no longer there, he was going to have to hire two men. Part of me felt guilty to be leaving him, but he never made me feel that way. I know he was proud of the fact that I wanted to go to school and pursue my own dreams.

My last day on the job was September 6th, 1963. We were adding a small brick extension to a house in Bensonhurst at the time. When we got in my father's truck to leave that day it was one of the strangest feelings I've ever had. Not getting up every morning and getting in the truck with my father, and not driving home with him every night was going to be a big change in my life. Working and driving together had made us very close. My father was not a man who was overly emotional or expressive, but if you spent enough time with him you learned to read him quite well. I knew by his body language, his expressions, and his hand movements, just what he was feeling. He taught me so much, not just about his craft, but also about how to conduct myself as a man and a person.

He didn't do it by preaching at me. Instead, he did

it the best way possible - by the example he set. He was a man of character, dignity, honesty and humility. He had pride and self respect, and he had his priorities straight.

He always put the people he loved ahead of himself. He wasn't much of a talker, but there were many times on the job, or driving in his truck, or at a ballgame, that my father would open up to me. It was almost as if he needed someone to talk to and to let out his feelings.

On that last day of work, I know my father was feeling a bit strange about it, too. We had worked together almost everyday for three years. Now it was suddenly going to end. Certainly I would work with him during vacations and in the summer, but that wasn't the same as spending eight or nine hours a day together for three years.

"What time you have to be at school tomorrow?" he asked as we drove home from Bensonhurst on that last day.

"My first class is at eleven, so I figure I'd leave about ten."

"What class is that?"

"Introduction to Mass Media."

"You wanna be a writer, eh?"

"Reporter, writer, photographer."

"It's gonna be strange not having you at the job."

"It's gonna be strange not being there."

"Whose chops am I gonna bust without you there?"

"You'll find somebody."

"You know Vincent, I think it's a really good thing

that you're doing this. No Anunnziato has ever gone to college, let alone graduate."

"You sure you're gonna be alright lugging bricks and stones around without me there?"

"What do you think I did before you started working with me?"

"You were a lot younger then."

"I got help, don't worry about it."

We drove in silence for a moment.

"How's things going with Rachel?" he asked.

"Good, Dad. It's just that she's going on that trip to Israel and I really don't want her to go."

"Does she want to go?"

"I think part of her does, and I think part of her is just going because her father wants her to."

"She's a really fine girl, Vincent. I hope things work out for you two. I really do."

"Thanks Dad, I appreciate that. I don't know if mom feels the same way."

"Mom likes Rachel a lot. You know that. I just think she's worried that if things really do work out between the two of you, you're gonna face some really tough choices. She just doesn't want to see you hurt or upset."

"I know."

"You nervous about starting school?"

"Not really, but I am a pretty old freshman."

"You'll do great, I know it."

"I'm looking forward to it, but I do feel a little guilty about leaving you on the job."

"Don't even think that, Vincent. You have nothing

to feel guilty about. Look, there comes a time when you have to do what you want to do. You don't want to be in the construction business. You want different things in life. That's okay. Me, I didn't have much of a choice. My father did it, he died, and I had to work to take care of the family. I went to war. When I came back, I had a wife and a son to support, and my mother. I did what I had to do and I don't regret the choices I made. But you always want better things for your kids. If you go to school and become a success at what you want to do, than that's what your mother and I want most for you. I hope you never have to touch another brick or cement block as long as you live."

"I have a feeling I'll be touching a few more bricks before I get out of school."

"Well sure, when you have the chance to work for me in the summer. But after you finish school, never again." He paused. "What did you two decide about telling her old man about you guys?"

"She's gonna tell him when she gets back from Israel."

"That's probably a good idea. Mr. Levy seemed like an okay guy in my dealings with him. He's just gonna have to deal with it I guess."

"I just think it's because he's so religious, you know.

"Seems that always gets in the way of things. To tell you the truth, every problem we ever had in this world, or probably ever will have, has to do with either religion or money, or both at the same time."

We pulled into the driveway of our house on Coney

Island Avenue. My father shut the engine and turned to me.

"Come on, get inside and get cleaned up. Me and you are going to the Mets game tonight. I got Ritigliano's tickets. They're playing the Braves."

Two hours later we were sitting at the Polo Grounds watching the Mets get absolutely pounded by the Milwaukee Braves. We were eating hotdogs and peanuts and drinking cokes. We never ate hot dogs and peanuts at home, only at games. As anyone who goes to ballgames knows, the ballpark franks are usually mushy masses of wet, pink meat and the peanuts are stale most of the time. Still, for some reason they tasted great at a ball game.

I tried to concentrate on the game, but all I could think about was the fact that Rachel was leaving for Israel in two weeks.

"Hey dad, how did you know mom was the one for you?" I asked as my father bit into a hot dog.

"What?"

"How did you know mom was the one?"

"Whatta you wanna know that for?"

"I don't know, just curious."

"You mother never told you how we ended up getting married?"

"I never asked her."

"Well, it was really her."

"Whatta you mean?"

"Well, you know your mother grew up down the street from me. She lived five doors down from where we live now. You know that."

"I know. Where Grandma Olimpia and Grandpa Mario still live."

"When we were little, say five or six, we were best friends. We always played together. Then, you know, as we got older, we grew apart. Hell, when you're eleven or twelve, all boys think girls are useless and all girls think boys are disgusting. Then, when we got into junior high and high school we became good friends again. Your mother was beautiful, just beautiful."

"Was she your girlfriend then?"

"No, not right away."

"You're confusing me here, dad."

"Vincent, your mother was beautiful and I really didn't think I had a shot with her. Sure, we were good friends, but I never thought she looked at me romantically or anything like that."

"Why not?"

"Look, Vincent, your mother was very popular in high school. All the best-looking guys in school asked her out. You know, the captain of the football team and guys like that. She went out on a lot of dates. Funny thing was, she never stayed with any of those guys. She never went steady with them or anything. I was in love with her even then. But who was I? I was just some short guy who barely got by in school and spent all his free time lugging bricks around for his old man."

I smiled. "Yeah, I know what that's like."

"Sure you do. But look, in high school you were much more popular and better lookin' than I was when I went to school. Plus, you were a football and baseball star. I was just some short, kinda chunky kid who happened to be good friends with your mom. I really never thought I had a shot with her as, you know, a boyfriend or anything."

"Well, obviously something happened. You got married."

My father smiled and took a gulp of his soda. "Well, that was really all your mom."

"Mom?"

"Yeah. See, in our senior year the prom was coming up and a lot of boys asked your mom to go with them, but she turned them all down. Me, I wasn't gonna go. I didn't have a girlfriend at the time and there wasn't anybody I was interested in askin'. So I just figured I wouldn't go."

"What happened?"

"Well, me and your mom was sitting in the lunchroom at school one day, about two weeks before the prom, and I asked her who she was goin' to the prom with. She told me that she didn't know. She said that a lot of boys had asked her, but not the right one. I said to her, 'Well, who's the right one?' She looked up at me and said, 'You, you idiot.' I'll tell you, you coulda knocked me over with a feather. We went to the prom together. It was really our first official date, and you know the rest of the story. We eventually got married. My old man died so I took over the business. We had you. Then the war came."

Just then we heard the crack of a bat and the crowd roared. "Marvelous" Marv Throneberry hit a homer for the Mets with two runners on base. The Mets now trailed in the game 11 to 3 in the sixth inning. They eventually lost the game by a score of 14 to 5.

"So if it wasn't for mom, I wouldn't be here," I said.

"That's right. Why you askin' me about all this stuff?"

"Like I said, just curious."

My father looked at me for a long moment. He knew I was thinking about Rachel, but he didn't say anything.

"It's different for everybody," he said. "I always loved your mother, since we were kids. I was just too stupid to say anything. Like I said, I didn't think I had a shot with her."

"But you were the one all along and mom knew it."

"Thank God for that. I guess I knew it, too"

"You were lucky."

"Yeah, I was. Best thing that ever happened to me. I can't explain it. I don't think anybody can. I guess you just know when it's the right person. You know, you just know when you know. Does that make any sense?"

"Yeah dad, believe it or not, it does."

The two weeks before Rachel left for Israel went by very quickly. We saw each other as much as we could. She was working in the city for her father, and with my schedule at school, it wasn't easy, but we made time whenever possible.

The day before she had to leave, we had dinner together in a little seafood place by the water in

Sheepshead Bay. Afterwards, we went and sat on a bench by the docks.

"I have to tell you something," I said.

"What?"

"You know the first time we really talked? That time you got off the bus and I was sitting on the bench reading a book?"

"Of course, you were reading *To Kill a Mockingbird."*

"I planned all that."

"All what?"

"That whole thing. I knew what time you came home, so I planned to be there when you got off the bus. I brought the book with me so you would be impressed."

"You know, I had a feeling at the time that you didn't spend many lunch hours reading great American novels."

"Before that day, I never did. It worked though, didn't it?"

"Yeah, it worked."

I looked at her. I couldn't for the life of me figure out what it was going to be like not seeing her for three weeks.

"I'm still not so happy with this Israel thing," I said.

"Do we have to go through this again? I'm leaving tomorrow."

"You could still tell your father that you just don't want to go. What's he gonna do? Disown you as a daughter?"

"I think he'd disown me as a daughter if he knew you and I have been seeing each other for a year."

"Rachel, if he loves you, and knows you love me, I still can't understand why we have to keep all this from him. It's been a year already. I know you said you'll tell him when you get back. But it just seems like this whole thing is crazy."

"You want to know something, Vincent? Something I've never told you?"

"What?"

"For the past year, every once and a while, I'd get home from work and my father would have a guest over for dinner. It was always some young Jewish guy. You know what he was trying to do?"

"Of course, trying to find a nice Jewish husband for you. Did he bring home anybody you were interested in?"

"How can you even say that?"

"I'm sorry. I'm just so upset about you going away. I still don't think you have to."

"Vincent, I've always done everything my father has asked of me."

"But you're a grown woman now. You need to start making your own choices."

"You're right, and I know you're right. I just feel like I have to do this one last thing for him. He was so proud that I was the first woman in the family to graduate college, and now he wants me to visit the Jewish homeland to understand and appreciate my heritage. I owe him that much. Like I said, when I get back from Israel we'll tell my father about us. That'll be the right time."

"I know what's gonna happen in Israel. You're

gonna meet some dashing Israeli guy and that's the end of us."

"Are you still worried about that?"

"I think about it every day."

"Stop thinking about it."

"I can't."

"Yes you can."

"No I can't, and wouldn't it make your old man happy if you came home in love with a nice Israeli boy."

"You don't have to be sarcastic."

"I don't know what else to be. My heart is breaking."

"Mine is, too."

"Seems to me you're all excited about this trip, like you don't care how I feel."

"Of course I'm a little excited about the trip. Am I not supposed to be? That doesn't mean I won't miss you horribly and think about you every minute I'm away."

"You'll be too busy with other stuff to be thinking about me."

"That's not true and you know it."

"No, I don't know it."

"If you don't know it by now, then maybe you never will."

"What's that supposed to mean? Does that mean you don't think I love you enough, so that gives you the opening to maybe look around for a nice Jewish boy in Israel?"

"Vincent, what exactly is going on in your head?"

"I wish I knew."

"I'm leaving tomorrow and we have to fight tonight?"

"What do you want me to do? Lie to you? Do I want you to go to Israel? No. Do I think that you might meet somebody else? Maybe. Do I think it's ridiculous that we've been together a year, even talked about getting married, and your father has no idea? Yes, it's ridiculous. I can't help what I'm feeling or thinking. It just is. Sometimes, when I think about all this stuff, I just get a horrible feeling in my stomach"

"Well don't you think that I think maybe you'll meet somebody when I'm away? Don't you think I know how you feel about my father's not knowing? I get that same feeling in my stomach."

"So then why are we bothering with all this?"

"Bothering with what?"

"Us."

"Now what are you saying? That we break up?"

"I didn't say that."

"I don't think you know what you're saying."

"Well, I guess I'm just one confused wop."

"There's nothing to be confused about. We love each other. I'll go away, I'll come back and we'll go on."

"As long as your old man don't find out before that, right?"

"We'll take care of that, too. I promise. As soon as I get back we'll tell him."

"We'll see."

"Vincent, look at me."

I kept staring down at my feet.

"Look at me, Vincent," she said.

I looked into her eyes.

"I love you," she said softly. "I gave you my heart and I gave you my body. No one has ever gotten those things except for you, and no one ever will. Do you understand me?"

"Yes."

She leaned over and kissed me.

"Just remember that when I'm away."

I nodded my head.

"We better get going," she said.

"I know."

We got in my father's car and drove in silence to Ocean Parkway. It was the same routine every time we went out. I'd drop her off about a block from her house so her father didn't see me. Then she'd walk from there. Her father always thought she was out with friends. I'd watch until she was safely in her front door.

On this night I pulled a little closer to the house and cut the engine.

"Okay, it's time," I said.

"Vincent, stop it now. This is our last night together before I go"

"We'll see each other tomorrow."

"I know, but I don't want to leave tonight when you're mad."

"I'll be fine."

"I know you, Vincent. You start thinking all these things in your head that are not really true, and you get all upset."

"Well, let's see. My girlfriend is gonna be thousands of miles away for three weeks. We're in love and have talked about getting married, but her father doesn't even know we're together. Jeez, I must be crazy to think these things."

"I can't talk to you when you get like this. We'll meet tomorrow at Stramiello's at eleven. I need to see you before I go. I have to see you. Then I have to get back to my house, because my dad is giving a little going away party for me at some kosher restaurant. Then we have to go to the airport, and I'll be thinking about nothing but you the entire time."

I looked over at her.

"You better get going," I said.

I leaned over and kissed her. She touched my face with her hand.

"You have nothing to worry about. I'll never love another man."

She got out of the car and walked toward her house. Tears welled up in my eyes as I watched her go.

When she got to her front door she turned toward the car and gave me a little wave, then walked in the door.

I sat there a few moments. I took a deep breath and drove off.

CHAPTER TWELVE

I didn't sleep well that night. I knew that the following day I would see Rachel for maybe an hour before she was gone for three weeks. I tossed and turned all night. I heard my father get up at six and leave the house by seven. For the three years prior I would have been going with him. I lay in bed and stared at the ceiling. At one point I thought I'd get up and go have coffee with the old man, but decided instead to just lie there. I had classes that day, but I had already decided to blow them off. I figured I'd see Rachel at eleven and then I'd be too depressed to do much of anything the rest of the day.

I drifted off to sleep at about eight and was in a deep sleep when I heard the phone ring. I looked at my alarm clock and saw that it was ten o'clock. I had to get up because I had to meet Rachel at the café at eleven. Then I heard my mother scream out, "Oh my God, no! Dear God in Heaven, no!"

I jumped from bed and ran into her bedroom. She hadn't even hung up the phone. She held it in her hand and was breathing heavily.

"Mom, what is it?" I asked.

It was if she didn't hear me. She stared straight ahead.

"Mom, what's going on?"

She looked up at me and started crying hysterically.

I knew at that moment that my father was dead.

I can't even recall in detail what happened over the next few hours. The only thing I remember clearly is going to Kings County Hospital where they took my father's body. I had to go officially identify him. My mother and sister wanted to come with me, but I wouldn't let them. I didn't want them to see my father lying dead on a table.

Before going to the hospital, I tried calling both Mole and Eyeballs to have them meet Rachel at the café to tell her what had happened. There was no answer at either of their houses. My mother and sister were crying hysterically. I had to get to the hospital to identify my father's body. I decided to call Rachel's house. If her father picked up the phone I'd just hang up, and if her mother did, I could explain the situation to her. The phone rang twice before Mr. Levy answered. I immediately hung up. I waited a few minutes and tried again. Once again Mr. Levy answered the phone. I waited about ten minutes and tried again.

"Hello? Hello?" Mr. Levy said.

This time I didn't hang up, but I didn't speak either.

"Who is this?" Mr. Levy said angrily into the phone. "Stop calling this number! I am taking the phone off the hook for now, whoever you are, so don't try calling again."

Then he slammed the phone down.

True to his word, Mr. Levy took the phone off the hook. When I tried again a few minutes later the line was busy. Now, I had no idea what to do.

I had to see how my mother and sister were doing and I had to get to the hospital. I decided to call Stramiello's Café and talk to Mrs. Stramiello. I could have her tell Rachel about my father when Rachel got there.

Mrs. S. wasn't in yet when I called the café, but her baker, Sergio, was working in the kitchen. Sergio had just come over from Sicily and barely spoke any English. I slowly told him what had happened, and asked him to have Mrs. S. tell Rachel.

"Yes, I tell Mrs. Stramiello to tell da girl you with you father," he said.

"Sergio, listen to me," I said. "Tell Mrs. S. that my father passed away and I had to go to the hospital, Capish? Tell her to tell Rachel when Rachel gets there. Capish? Rachel can't come to my house. I won't be here. I'll be at the hospital. Capish?"

"Si, si, I tell. I tell. You go to you father"

I got to the hospital around eleven and a doctor led me to the morgue where my father lay. That image was burned into my brain and will never leave me. He was on a metal table covered with a white sheet. They pulled the sheet back. His eyes were shut and his face was frozen in a mask of pain. I just nodded when I saw him and they covered him up again.

The doctor said it was a massive heart attack. The man who was working with dad that day, a guy named Sam, said he saw my father lift a heavy wheelbarrow full of bricks, which was usually my job. Sam then turned back to what he was doing, and when he turned again to see where my father was with the bricks, he saw him lying on the ground next to the wheelbarrow.

The doctor said the coronary was so massive that he was most likely dead before he hit the ground.

Rachel walked in the door of Stramiello's Café at about five minutes to eleven. Mrs. Stramiello greeted her with a kiss and a hug. Rachel and Vincent had come to the café many times during the past year. Rachel sat down at one of the tables and Mrs. Stramiello sat opposite her.

"Rachel," said Mrs S., "Vincenzo, he call this morning and say he had to go to his father. So he no come here."

Rachel suddenly felt an empty feeling in the pit of her stomach. "When did he call?" she asked.

"He call this morning. I no here. Sergio answer da phone and tell me to tell you dat Vincent have-a to be with his father this morning."

"Did he say why?"

"No, Sergio just tell me that Vincenzo with his father. Dat's all he say. Sergio no speak da English so well.

"I'm leaving today for Israel. Vincent is supposed to meet me here."

"I'm-a sure he has da good reason to be with his father. You stay, maybe he come late. You wanna eat somethin'?"

"No thanks, I'll just wait awhile."

"Good, I bring-a you some coffee."

Rachel waited an hour and at twelve she knew for sure Vincent wasn't coming. She thought about walking to Vincent's house but realized there wasn't enough time. She had to be back at her house by 12:30. Her father was taking the family out to the finest kosher restaurant in Brooklyn for Rachel's farewell lunch. From there they were going straight to the airport. She was worried but also hurt, and she was mad. Maybe something was wrong. She had no idea what to think. She walked to the counter where Mrs. S. stood.

"Mrs. S.," said Rachel, "if Vincent comes by please tell him I was here."

"You leave now?"

"I have to go. Please tell him I was here if you see him."

"Sure, sure."

Rachel walked home with tears in her eyes. She didn't know what to think. When she got home she sneaked upstairs and called Vincent's house. The line was busy. She hung up and called again thinking that maybe she had dialed the wrong number. The line was still busy. She hung up the phone and when she did she noticed she was wearing the bracelet Vincent gave her. She took it off and put it in the pocket of her dress.

It wasn't until the day my father died that I fully understood what a strong woman my mother was. Yes, she was devastated, but she also took charge of everything.

My kid sister, Marie, who was then sixteen, was hysterical for most of the first day. My mother spent hours with her trying to ease Marie's pain. I had to stay at the hospital until about 12:30 because I had to fill out all kinds of paperwork to have them bring my father's body to the funeral home.

When I got home a little before one o'clock I called Rachel's house. At that point I just didn't care if her father answered the phone. I knew her father was taking the family out to some kosher restaurant for Rachel's farewell lunch. I had no idea what restaurant it was and I was hoping to catch them before they left. I had to talk to her and tell her what had happened and why I hadn't met her. We hadn't left off on the best of terms the night before, and I had been a jerk. I wanted to tell her I loved her and trusted her, and to think of me always when she was in Israel. When I called I braced myself for her father to answer the phone. Nobody answered. They had already left.

I had never felt so helpless in my life.

I ran down to Stramiello's to make sure Mrs. S. had told Rachel what had happened with my dad. Mrs. S. didn't even know that my father had passed away. It seems the only part of my phone message that Sergio understood was that I couldn't be at the café to meet Rachel because I was with my father, and that's what Mrs. S. told Rachel. So Rachel didn't even know my father had died. I couldn't even imagine what Rachel was thinking at that point. Did she think I just didn't show up because I decided to work for my father that day? She must know better than that. She must know I would never do anything like that.

When I returned home from the café I spent the next few hours calling relatives and friends to tell them the bad news about my father. I also made all the arrangements with the funeral home and the cemetery. I ordered food. It was good to be busy as it took my mind off my own grief.

Rachel was trying to act happy and cheerful at her going-away party, but it was difficult. All she could think about was Vincent. Why hadn't he come to Stramiello's? Something must be wrong.

Rachel's relatives and family friends all came by to wish her well on her trip and to tell her how lucky she was to be going on such a wonderful journey. She smiled and thanked everybody, but her heart wasn't in it. She wanted to see Vincent, or at least talk to him. But there was nothing she could do. She had never felt so helpless in life.

At three o'clock the party ended and Rachel got in the car with her father, mother and two younger brothers to drive to Idlewild Airport. She had made up her mind that when she got there she was going to tell her father she had use the bathroom, then sneak off and try to call Vincent one more time. She needed to hear his voice one more time before she left. She needed to tell Vincent she loved him

Her plane departed at five.

I knew Rachel's plane left at five. By three o'clock my house was filled with relatives and friends. My father's wake was to begin the next day and last for two days, with the funeral on Saturday. At around four o'clock I got a call from the funeral home. I needed to bring them one of my father's suits for him to be laid out in.

After leaving the funeral home, I thought about driving to the airport to see Rachel. I didn't care if her family saw me. I wanted her to know what had happened and why I hadn't met her. Then I suddenly realized that I didn't even know what airline she was on.

Just before Rachel boarded the plane at four o'clock, she sneaked off and called Vincent's house. The line was busy again. She tried three more times. The line was still busy. On her fifth try, a woman answered the phone whose voice she didn't recognize. It wasn't Mrs. Annunziato or Vincent's sister, Maria. The woman spoke with a very heavy Italian accent.

"Is Vincent there?" Rachel asked.

"Vincent no here. He need to bring clothes for his father," the woman said.

"When he gets back, please tell him Rachel called."

"Sure, sure, I tell."

The woman hung up abruptly.

Rachel's mother knew something was bothering her daughter. She took Rachel into the ladies room to talk.

Rachel told her that Vincent was supposed to meet her to say good-bye, but didn't show up at the café.

"That's just not like him," said Rachel.

"Do you think something is wrong?"

"I don't know, mom. I don't know what to think."

"Do you want me to call Vincent's house when I get home?"

"No, I'll call him when I get to Israel."

"I'm sure everything is okay, sweetheart. I'm sure there's a good reason why he didn't meet you this morning."

As Rachel settled into her seat on the plane, she knew in her heart that something was dreadfully wrong. She could just feel it. Vincent would have been at Stramiello's unless there was something that kept him from being there. She knew that as well as she knew anything in this world. She had a sick feeling in the pit of her stomach. She made up her mind to call him when she landed in Israel. She had to at least hear his voice. She reached into the pocket of her dress and took out the bracelet Vincent had given her. She clasped it on to her right wrist. She closed her eyes and pictured the smile on Vincent's face when he gave it to her. It made her smile even though her heart was breaking.

She landed in Tel Aviv nine hours later. It was eleven o'clock the next day already in Israel. She took a bus to her hotel and checked in at about noon. She wanted to call Vincent's house immediately, but realized it was five o'clock in the morning in New York. She decided to make the call at four in the afternoon Israeli time, this way it would be nine in the morning in New York. She knew Vincent left for school at ten.

Family and friends came to our house all afternoon on the day my father died. I greeted everybody as they came in the door and accepted their condolences. I was numb, just numb. I did what needed to be done, but I was in a shocked daze the whole time.

My thoughts jumped back and forth between memories of my father and visions of Rachel. I knew the next three days would be the toughest of my life. My father would be waked for two days at the funeral home, followed by his funeral and burial on Saturday. Other thoughts flashed in my head. What about college now? Did I have to quit to take over my father's business? How would my mom and kid sister live if I didn't take over the business? I was confused, angry and heartbroken.

I knew the one thing I had to do was write Rachel a letter and mail it as soon as possible. I had no idea how long it took for a letter to get to Israel from Brooklyn. She had given me the address and phone number of the hotel she was staying at her first night in Israel. The following morning she was leaving for the kibbutz near the city of Haifa. The kibbutz had no phone service. I did, however, have her address at the kibbutz.

I had to let her to know what had happened. Most of all, I just wanted to tell her I loved her and I would be there waiting for her when she came home.

I knew Rachel's flight took nine hours. It would be eleven o'clock in the morning the next day in Israel when she landed. I figured she'd be in her hotel by one o'clock at the latest. With the seven-hour time difference, if I called her at six in the morning New York time, it'd be one in the afternoon in Israel. That night I set my alarm so I'd wake up at six to call Rachel.

After setting my alarm, I sat on my bed and wrote her a letter. I intended to mail it on Thursday morning before going to the funeral home for the first day of my father's wake.

At six in the morning my alarm went off and I called Rachel's hotel in Israel. There was no answer in her room. I left a message that I would call back later.

After checking into her hotel, Rachel rested for a short while then decided to take a walk through downtown Tel Aviv. She had to wait at least three hours before she called Vincent at four that afternoon. She left her room at about ten minutes to one.

When she returned to the hotel two hours later there was a message for her at the main desk. She found out that Vincent had called and would try again later. For the first time since she left New York she felt joy. I am going to talk to Vincent in a few hours, she thought. I'm not going to wait for him to call, instead I'm going to call him at four o'clock Israeli time

At the stroke of four o'clock, she put the call

through to Vincent's house. There was no answer. She could not have known that the whole family was at Mr. Annunziato's wake.

Before going to my father's wake I stopped by the post office and sent Rachel her letter via airmail. At midnight on that same day I made another call to Rachel's hotel. It was seven o'clock in the morning in Israel, and I knew Rachel was leaving for the kibbutz that morning.

When I got through to the hotel I was told that Rachel had already checked out.

Rachel had to be on the bus to the kibbutz by seven in the morning. She had checked out of the hotel at 6:30 and sat in the lobby waiting for the bus. Vincent still hadn't called back. She wanted more than anything to call New York, but felt it would be rude of her to call the Anunnziato house at midnight New York time.

Finally, after debating it in her mind, she decided she would call Vincent before she got on the bus.
She had to hear his voice. She was sure Mrs. Anunnziato would understand when the ringing phone woke everybody up in the middle of the night.

There was only one phone in the hotel lobby on which international calls could be made. Luckily, there was no one using that phone. She went over and dialed Vincent's number.

The line was busy.

As she listened to the busy signal she glanced over at the hotel operator who was behind the main desk only about twenty feet away from her. She could hear what the operator was saying.

"I am sorry, sir, but Miss Rachel Levy has already checked out of the hotel. No, I'm sorry, there is no way for me to contact her."

Rachel suddenly realized as she listened to the hotel operator that the operator was talking to Vincent. She just knew it. It was almost midnight in New York. Who else would be calling her at midnight? Certainly not her parents. She knew that's why Vincent's phone was busy. He was calling her in Israel! Rachel hung up the phone and raced toward the operator.

"Please wait!" Rachel said as she ran toward the hotel operator

The operator hung up the phone just as Rachel reached the front desk.

"I'm Rachel Levy," said Rachel. "Was that Vincent Anunnziato on the phone?"

The operator looked down at her message pad. "Yes, a Mr. Vincent, ah........calling from Brooklyn in the United States."

"Can you get him back on the line?" asked Rachel.

"No, I am sorry young lady. I am not permitted to make outgoing international calls for guests on this line. You have to use the international line you were just on."

"Can you make an exception just this once?"

"No, I'm sorry, you must use international line in

the lobby," she said as she pointed to the phone Rachel had just hung up.

Rachel turned toward the international phone just a few feet from where she stood. A man was using it and there were two people waiting on line behind him. It would be at least an hour, maybe more, before she could use that phone again. The bus for the kibbutz was leaving in ten minutes. Rachel thought about pleading with the first man in line to see if he would allow her to make her call before him. But she only had ten minutes before the bus left and it would probably take that long to get through to Brooklyn.

That's it, she thought

There were no phones on the kibbutz where she was going. If she was going to talk to Vincent sometime over the next three weeks she'd have to go into the city of Haifa to do so. Haifa was only a few miles from the kibbutz. She made up her mind she would find a way

---

More than 500 people attended my father's wake over a two-day period. There was a viewing during the day from eleven to five, and then another at night from seven to ten. It was packed every time. In between sessions on each day, people came back to our house to eat. The food was plentiful. Everybody made something and brought it over. Italians celebrate life with food and also mourn death with it. There was so much food that I had to bring a lot of it to our neighbor's houses to keep in their refrigerator. The funeral director was sure that my father must have been some big wig in the mob. He had never seen so many people except at wakes for big shot Mafioso.

I was astonished at my mother's strength. She greeted everybody and had a word with every one of them as they came by to pay their respects. It was only at night at home that my mother broke down. I could hear her weeping softly in her room. My kid sister also showed remarkable strength. I had always kind of seen her as my bratty little sister. But now I looked at her and saw a young woman. She helped my mother through everything. I was so proud of her and I told her so. I told her how proud our father would have been. I could hear her cry at night as well. I don't know if they heard me crying.

I gave the eulogy at my Dad's funeral. I stood at the pulpit of our church. My mom and sister were in the first row in front of me. Mole and Eyeballs sat next to them. There were over four hundred people in the church.

"I thought a lot about what I was going to say today," I said. "You know, it's hard to sum up a man's life in a few words. When I think about my dad, I realize how lucky I was that he was my father. I learned so much from him. I learned about commitment and responsibility. I learned about hard work, perseverance, humility, dedication, loyalty, all those things and so much more. Mostly, I guess, I learned from my dad, and my mom, that you always put the people you love ahead of yourself. I know from them that that's what real love is all about.

"The thing I most respected, loved and admired about my dad was that he always knew what the important things in life were, and what wasn't so important. I guess you could say he had his priorities straight. He never let things he couldn't control get to him. I don't think I ever saw him really lose his temper. Except maybe one time when I was about eight or nine. I got mad at my mother for something, and I cursed at her in Italian. I didn't even know what the Italian curse word meant. All I know is that my dad grabbed me by the arm, dragged me upstairs to my room, and told me I was to never speak like that to my mom again, and for that matter, never speak like that to any adult.

"You see, my father really appreciated the special moments in life. Being with his family on the holidays. Seeing my sister or me in a school play, or seeing me play baseball. Or just sitting down as a family for dinner. He knew that those were the times we would all remember most. He was right. He usually was.

"My father was a great teacher. He never lectured me about anything. Instead he taught me by the example of how he lived his life. For as long as I can remember, my father got up at six in the morning to go to work. I'm sure there were mornings when he just didn't want to get up. But he always did because that was how he took care of his family. It didn't matter if it was raining or snowing or one hundred degrees outside, my dad went to work. There were times when he was so sick he should have never gotten out of bed. I remember my mom pleading with him to stay home and get better, but dad went to work.

"For the last three years I've been working with my dad. I saw how he dealt with his customers. He was always fair and patient, even when the customers were maybe being jerks.

"Most of you know that my dad wasn't the most talkative guy around. He never said much, and I think that maybe he had trouble sometimes expressing what he felt in his heart. I think that came from his experiences in the war. He never talked about it much. One time when I was a little kid I overheard him telling the widow of a friend how that friend died in combat at Normandy. And just a few months ago, my dad told me a little about what it was like to be in a war on the front lines. Those are the only two times I ever remember dad talking about the war. But I have read about some of the battles my dad fought in. He must have seen hundreds, maybe even thousands of his fellow soldiers die. I'm sure he must have seen so many horrible things, that he just wanted to forget all about it and try to get back to some kind of normal life with my mom when he came home from overseas. But he could never forget completely, and I think that shaped the kind of man he was. I guess I understand now that after all the horrors he saw in war he felt lucky to be alive, and that every day of his life after that was a gift and a blessing, and that's how he lived his life.

"I'm sure most of you don't know this, but my dad won a Silver Star for bravery in combat in Italy. My mother didn't even know about it for many years. The only reason we found out was that I found the Silver Star in a box in the attic one day when I was about 13 or 14. I asked my dad what it was, and he said it was just something he got in the army. That was it. My mom explained to me that it was a medal for bravery. I was very proud of that. My dad a war hero, but I never asked him what he did to win that medal. I kind of knew he wouldn't want to talk about it.

"On the day my father died I heard him get up at six in the morning to go to work like he always did. I was awake and I thought that maybe I'd get up and have a cup of coffee with him. Instead, I decided to stay in bed. I had classes that day and was pretty tired. I just figured I would see him at dinner that night. I wish now that I had gotten up. I wish a lot of things now. I wish I had told my dad more how much I loved him - and how much I respected and admired him.

"When I was little I would always hug and kiss my dad and tell him I loved him. But as you get older that kind of stops. I guess maybe every father and son go through that. I wish now that on the day he died I had gotten up and gone down to the kitchen to have coffee with him. I wish I had the chance to tell him that I love him, and how lucky and fortunate I feel that he was my father. I wish I could thank him for all that he taught me and all the sacrifices he made for me and my sister and my mom. But I'll never have that chance again. I know I'll regret that for the rest of my life.

"I guess in the end the true measure of a man's life is not what he did for himself, but how he touched the lives of other people. In that way, my dad was a great man. He touched so many lives in a good way, and that's why you're all here to pay your respects today.

"I know that dad's in Heaven now, and I know he's looking down, and he wouldn't be very happy with what he sees here today. The last thing that dad would ever want to see in this world was his family and friends in pain. What he wanted most in life was for the people that he loved to be happy. If my dad was here I know he'd appreciate everybody paying tribute to him, but he'd also say that enough is enough. He'd tell us to go home, have my mom make some ziti with meat sauce, which was his favorite, bring out the gallon of red wine, and instead of mourning his death, we should celebrate his life. That's what my dad would tell us to do today......Don't mourn his death. Celebrate his life."

People told me it was a beautiful tribute, but I still felt within myself that it was impossible to find the words to describe what he meant to me. We buried him that afternoon at St. Charles Cemetery on Long Island. All our deceased family members were buried there. After my father's funeral I visited my grandfather's grave. It was my father's father and I was named after him. It was strange to see the name Vincenzo Anunnziato on a tombstone.

After the funeral the whole family came to my house to eat and pay their final respects. It was good to have so many people around – uncles, aunts, cousins, and friends. It was more a celebration of my father's life than a mourning of his death. That's what he would have wanted.

Later that night, after everybody had left the house, I went down to the kitchen to get something to drink. It was about ten o'clock and only the nightlight was on in the kitchen. My mother was sitting at the table. She was drinking a glass of milk.

"What's the matter, baby?" she asked as I came in the kitchen. "Couldn't sleep?"

"No, I was just thirsty."

"Have some soda. It's in the fridge."

I got myself a bottle of cold Coca-Cola and sat at the table with my mom.

"Now what, ma?"

"Don't worry, Vincent, we'll get through this."

"I guess I'll stop school for now and take over for dad."

"No Vincent, that's not what your father would have wanted."

"I know, ma, but somebody's got to take over. He has four jobs lined up that need to be done, plus, how are we gonna live without the income from the business?"

"Your father took care of that."

"What are you talking about?"

"I said your father already took care of that."

"How?"

"Well, we hadn't said anything to you kids yet, but after you graduated college next year, dad was gonna retire. He made arrangements to sell the business to Sam, the man who works with you once and a while. I talked to Sam at the wake, and he said he'd be willing to start making his payments for the business next month. So we'll get a good amount of money for that, and he can do the jobs your father had lined up. Plus your father put away a good amount of money over the years. It was for our retirement. He also had a large life insurance policy in case anything happened to him. He always wanted to make sure that we were all taken care of. And there's more than enough money in your college account for you to finish school. So you don't have to quit school and work."

I didn't think it was possible for me to love and respect my father more than I did. But sitting at that table and hearing what my mother told me just made me shake my head in awe at the kind of man he was. I was grief-stricken by his death, but at that moment also felt so lucky to have had him for the years that I did.

"Vincent, you have to understand something about dad. He was not a rich man and maybe he wasn't always so good at expressing the things he felt in his heart, but he knew what was important in life. His family always came first above everything else, especially you and your sister. I knew that you would come to me to tell me that you were going to quit school to take over the business. I knew that because you are so much like your father in so many ways. But because of him, you don't have to. You go to school, baby. You follow your dreams. That's what your father would have wanted more than anything."

After my mother told me this, all the emotion that had been locked up inside of me for three days burst out. I started to cry and couldn't stop myself. My mother came and sat next to me and held me in her arms. It felt like I was a little boy again and the protection and love I felt in my mother's arms was what I needed most at that moment.

When I caught my breath and wiped my eyes, my mom asked me if I was okay.

"I'm okay, ma. Sorry about that."

"You have nothing to be sorry for."

"Ma, if I had been there, then dad wouldn't have been pushing that wheelbarrow and he'd still be here."

"You don't know that. You can't blame yourself. Vincent, your father was so proud of you. He bragged to everybody about you. He couldn't tell enough people that his son was going to college. Only a week ago we were sitting in bed reading and he just leaned over and kissed me. I said, 'What was that for?' He said, 'Because of the wonderful children you've raised.' I told him that we had raised you two together and he deserved as much credit as I did. He smiled and told me that of all he had done in his life - fighting in the war, building a business, all of that - the thing he was most proud of was the man you had become and the woman your sister was becoming."

"I hope I can be the man he was."

"You already are Vincent."

I had to swallow hard to keep from crying again.

"I'm sorry Vincent, I forgot to ask you if you got to see Rachel before she left."

"No ma, I didn't get to see her. I was supposed to meet her at Stramiello's the day dad died. I called there and told Sergio to tell her what had happened. But, you know, he doesn't speak English that well, and the only part of the message he got was that I couldn't be there because I was with dad. That's what Mrs. S. told Rachel, so Rachel doesn't even know about dad. She must think I'm a real jerk for not showing up."

"Well then, call her now. Do you know where's she staying?"

"Yeah, she was at a hotel her first night, but then she was leaving the next morning to go work on a kibbutz out in the country. They don't have any phones at her kibbutz. I called her hotel twice, but the first time there was no answer in her room, and the second time she had checked out already."

"Do you have her address?"

"Yeah, I wrote her a letter and mailed it on Thursday. I have no idea how long it's gonna take to get to her."

"Do you think her parents know how to get in touch with her?"

"I don't know. It wouldn't matter anyway. Her father still doesn't know we've been seeing each other. She told me her mother knows, but not her old man."

"When does she plan on telling him?"

"When she gets back from Israel."

"I guess she knows best when to do it."

"Ma, not for nothing, but I always kind of felt like you weren't crazy about me and Rachel being together. I mean, I know you liked her well enough after you got to know her, but I still thought you were kind of against it."

"First off, Vincent, whatever makes you happy

makes me happy. You're my child. I want to see you happy. And you know something? What does it matter who you love? Love is a good thing and there sure isn't enough of it in this world."

Rachel hated working on the kibbutz. It wasn't the hard work that bothered her, it was the boredom. Every morning she awoke and got on a truck with dozens of other people. They were driven out into the fields where they spent ten hours a day picking pears in the blistering hot sun. At night she was far too exhausted to do anything but eat dinner and go to sleep.

She lived in a small wooden cabin with two other American girls, one from Boston and the other from Philadelphia. Both were as bored as Rachel was. Living on the kibbutz was like living in the dark ages. There were no telephones, just a radio that was used to contact Haifa if there was an emergency on the kibbutz. The entire settlement consisted of nothing but dozens of wooden buildings and hundreds of acres of pear orchids. There were communal bathrooms that had running water, but no toilets. The women had to squat over deep holes in the ground with wooden handles on each side to hold on to. Everybody had to wash their clothes in big tubs and hang them on clotheslines to dry. The clothes dried very quickly in the blazing sun, but Rachel soon found out that she had to watch her things carefully. One day, two of her work dresses were missing from the line when she went to get them. Somebody had obviously taken them and whoever did wasn't going to wear them until Rachel left. She had brought only one small suitcase. It was all she was allowed to bring. She didn't have many clothes with her to begin with. After her dresses were stolen she started to dry her laundry on a bench outside her cabin to make sure nothing disappeared.

There was electric on the kibbutz, but it was monitored very closely. At nine o'clock every night the power was shut down except for a few lights to guide people to the outhouses in the middle of the night. If someone wanted to read at night they needed a flashlight. Sometimes there were social gatherings scheduled on certain nights, but most people were just too exhausted to attend.

Married couples, or families with children, were given their own small wooden cabins to live in, but everybody else lived three or four people to a cabin. The beds in the cabins were just metal frame cots. All meals were served in a communal dining hall. The food was horrendously bad, and sometimes Rachel would smile when she thought about what Vincent would think of the food they had to eat. Mail was delivered to the kibbutz twice a week by truck.

Rachel respected the people who lived on the kibbutz. After all, through incredibly hard work, they had turned the desert into a fertile orchid. Still, the people who lived there were not very friendly to the volunteer workers. There were about twenty volunteers in all, mostly from America, but some from

Europe as well. Rachel felt as if the people who lived on the kibbutz looked at the volunteers as nothing more than free labor for however long they were there. They made no effort to make the volunteers feel especially welcome.

In fact, most of the people on the kibbutz viewed the American volunteers as spoiled and pampered rich kids who had trouble handling the manual labor of kibbutz life. Rachel could see that this was true of the Americans in many cases. She however did not feel that way about her roommates or herself. They never complained and worked as hard as they could.

On Rachel's first day working in the orchids she was wearing the bracelet Vincent had given her. While pulling a pear off a tree the bracelet got snagged on a branch and was almost torn off her wrist. From that day forward she took off the bracelet in the morning and put it in her suitcase before heading to the fields, but she always put it back on when she returned to her cabin in the evening.

Picking pears in the fields all day gave Rachel too much time to think. It was mind-numbing work. All she did was think about Vincent. She wondered what he was doing. She wondered if he missed her as much as she missed him. She wondered if he still loved her as she did him. She wondered how he was doing in school. Maybe Vincent was right. Maybe she should have told her father that she just didn't want to come to Israel. After her first few days there all she wanted to do was go home. She wondered time and time again why Vincent hadn't met her on the morning she left for Israel. There had to be a good reason.

The only way for her to call Vincent on the phone was to take the bus into Haifa. But even then, she was told, the chances of getting through to America were very, very slim. Besides, because Israeli time was seven hours ahead of New York time, she'd have to go into Haifa in the evening to make the call to catch Vincent in the morning. She was advised, however, that traveling at night was not safe. There was much tension in the area between the Palestinian Arabs who lived there and the Israeli settlers. Rachel had seen detachments of Israeli soldiers with automatic weapons patrolling the area on a regular basis. It scared her to see soldiers carrying these weapons and she hoped she would not witness any kind of violent confrontation between the Israeli soldiers and the Palestinians. She had heard stories of "incidents" where groups of young Palestinians attacked Israeli settlers with stones while they worked in remote areas of the orchids.

Despite the danger, Rachel had already made two trips into Haifa in the evening to try and call Vincent during her first week on the kibbutz. She had to go to the Haifa Phone Company building where they had a room set up with ten phones on which international calls could be made. Both times she had to wait in line for over an hour to use a phone. The first time she couldn't get a line through to New York despite numerous attempts. The second time she went she was happy to see that there was no line at all to use the phones. The reason there were no people waiting in line was because the entire Haifa phone system had completely broken down.

A gang of young Palestinians had chopped down two telephone poles to block off the main road in and out of the city. This had caused the whole phone system in Haifa to go down. When a bus leaving Haifa came to the blockade, the Palestinians began throwing rocks at the bus. Fortunately an Israeli army patrol arrived quickly at the scene. The Palestinians fled and no one on the bus was injured.

Rachel had spoken to her parents only once, when she had arrived at the hotel in Tel Aviv. She also sent them a telegram from Haifa when she arrived there. She had thought about sending Vincent a telegram as well, but how could she tell him what she was feeling in her heart with just a few lines in a telegram? All she knew for sure was that she loved him with all her heart and missed him desperately.

"Hey Bricks, are you okay?" Mole asked me.

We were at the playground shooting baskets. It was Friday afternoon. I had no classes that day. Every morning since the day my father died and Rachel left for Israel, I'd wake up and the reality of my world would hit me hard. I'd get an empty, sick feeling in the pit of my stomach. It had been ten days since my father died. The thought of never seeing him again, never talking to him again was just so difficult for me to accept. Seeing my mother and sister so heartbroken broke my heart, and there was nothing I could do about it. I hated that helpless feeling.

Then I'd think about Rachel. She had been in Israel for ten days, but it seemed like a month to me. I missed her so much and the thought of not seeing her for another two weeks was almost too much to bear. What did she think when I didn't show up at the café to say good-bye? Did she think I didn't love her anymore? Did she think that was my way of ending our relationship? In her heart she must somehow know that I would never do anything like that. If I could only talk to her. Why didn't she call me? I knew the kibbutz had no phones, but there had to be a way for her to get to a phone. She could call collect for all I cared. Maybe she just didn't want to talk to me. I had no idea what to think. I was one miserable Italian.

"Hey Bricks," Mole said.

"What?"

"Are you doing okay?"

"Ah shit, Mole, I just got so many things on my mind."

"How's your mom and sister doing?"

"I guess as good as they can. It's been real tough on them."

"You too, Bricks, you too."

"Well, at least my sister and I have school to keep our minds off things. My mother is in the house all day. She has too much time to think."

"Maybe she should get a job or something, you know, to get her out of the house."

"I know, I told her that. I just don't think she's ready yet."

"Maybe you have to push her a little bit."

"To tell you the truth, Mole, sometimes I really don't know what to do. Ten days ago I had a father and a girl I loved, now my father's dead and Rachel is thousands of miles away and I have no idea what she's thinking. Maybe she thinks I'm a complete asshole for not showing up to say good-bye to her. I told you what happened with Sergio, and him screwing up my message, so Rachel doesn't even know my father passed away that morning. What a friggin' nightmare"

"Did you try and call her?"

"Yeah, I tried calling her at her hotel but I didn't get her. Then she left for the kibbutz.

"The what?"

"The kibbutz."

"What the hell is a kibbutz?"

"It's like these huge farms they have in Israel, and hundreds of people work and live on the kibbutz. Rachel is there working for three weeks."

"So call her there."

"They don't have phones. This place is way the hell out in the country somewhere. I wrote her a letter, but I don't know how long it takes to get there. The guy at the post office said maybe nine or ten days if I was lucky."

"So, send her a telegram."

"What?"

"Send her a telegram. I'm sure you can do that."

"You know, I didn't think of that."

"Of course not. That's why I'm here, to do your

thinking for you."

"How much can you write in a telegram?"

"I have no clue," said Mole. "I never sent one, but I think you can send a couple of lines."

"You know, that might work."

"Sure."

"Then let's go."

I tossed the basketball to Mole and started walking up the block toward my house.

"Hey Bricks, what the hell are you doing?"

"I'm going to my house to look in the phone book for the nearest Western Union place, then you're driving me there so I can send Rachel a telegram."

One hour later Mole and I were standing in a Western Union office on Atlantic Avenue in downtown Brooklyn. I sent Rachel a telegram.

Saturday was the Sabbath so there was no work on the kibbutz. On Sunday, Rachel had the day off and decided in the morning to take the bus into Haifa to do some shopping. She bought souvenirs for her younger brothers and two new work dresses to replace the ones that had been stolen. She looked in a number of different shops to find something for Vincent, but really didn't see anything he might like. She decided to go to the international phone center again to call Vincent despite the fact that it was the middle of the night in New York.

When she arrived at the phone company building the line of people was out the door. She was told there was over a three-hour wait to use one of the international phone lines. She decided to head back to the kibbutz. She would try calling Vincent again early next week.

The work on the kibbutz was boring, but the days Rachel had off were even more boring. There was just nothing to do. Because of the daily manual labor in the orchids, Rachel was constantly tired. Her plan for Sunday was to take an afternoon nap, sit in the sun a while, eat dinner, and get to bed early for work on Monday.

When she got back to the kibbutz she walked into her cabin and saw two envelopes on her cot. Her heart jumped. She just knew they were from Vincent. One was a Western Union envelope and the other an airmail envelope. Her roommates were still in Haifa so she had the cabin to herself.

She dropped the bags she was carrying and raced to her cot. She sat down and picked up the envelopes. She immediately recognized Vincent's handwriting on the airmail envelope. Her heart was filled with both joy and dread. Seeing his letter made her happier than she had ever been, but what did the letter say? A part of her was afraid to open the letter. She stared at it. The postmark said September 22nd, the day after she had left for Israel. Finally she took a deep breath and opened it.

September 21, 1963
Dear Rachel,

My father died this morning. That's why I didn't meet you

at the café. He had a massive heart attack while working. The doctor at the hospital told me he was probably dead before he hit the ground. I tried calling Mole and Eyeballs to have them meet you to tell you what had happened, but neither one of them was home. I called the café and told Sergio what had happened, and he was supposed to tell Mrs. S. to tell you. But Sergio screwed up the message and I found out from Mrs. S. that all she told you was I couldn't be there because I was with my father. I can't even imagine what you thought when you heard that.

At the time I was supposed to meet you, I was at the hospital identifying my father's body. Then I had to get back home to take care of things for my mother and sister. I spent most of this morning and afternoon calling relatives and friends to tell them the bad news.

I called your house at about one o'clock. I didn't care if your father answered the phone. I had to talk to you to tell you what had happened. There was no answer, so I knew you had already left for the restaurant.

Had I known what restaurant you were at or what airline you were on, I swear I would have driven to see you this afternoon, or at least I would have tried to reach you by phone. I wouldn't have cared if your father saw me. I felt so helpless.

It's about six in the morning now, so I guess it's about one in the afternoon in Israel. I called your hotel just a little while ago, but there was no answer in your room. I'll try again later.

I wish I could write more, but I am so tired and so heartbroken it's very difficult for me to express in words what I feel. I do feel the worst sense of loss I have ever felt in my life. I know I will miss my father every day for as long as

I live. The pain is almost too much to bear. And not being able to see you, to hold you, to kiss you, just makes it worse. I just want you to know I love you with all my heart, I will miss you every single day you are gone, and I will be waiting for you when you come home.

I Love You,
Vincent

In her entire life Rachel had never felt such joy and such sorrow at the same time. Tears filled her eyes and dropped on to the pages of Vincent's letter. Vincent loves me, she thought. He will be there when I return. She couldn't ask for anything more. Her heart was full. At the same time her heart ached because of the pain she knew Vincent must have been feeling. All she wanted to do is be there for him. To hold him when he cried. To comfort him. She, too, felt helpless. She was thousands of miles away on the other side of the world. She would be in Israel fourteen more days. She knew they would be the longest days of her life.

She folded Vincent's letter, put it back in the envelope and put it in her suitcase. She then picked up the envelope with the telegram in it.

Rachel:
My father died the day you left. That's why I didn't meet you. I love you and will be here when you get back. Sent letter to you.

Vincent

Rachel fell back on her pillow and began to cry She cried for many hours before she drifted off to sleep.

On Monday morning the truck was waiting outside to take Rachel and her roommates to the orchids for a day of picking pears. She told the driver she was ill and would not be going that day. As soon as her roommates left, Rachel sat on her cot to write a letter to Vincent. His letter took eleven days to get to her. If she wrote him today and gave it to the mail truck driver when he came tomorrow, then it should arrive in Brooklyn before she got home. She had to tell Vincent what she was feeling. She had to tell him how much she loved him and how much she grieved for him. She felt as if she would burst if she didn't let her feelings out. Even if she arrived home in Brooklyn before the letter did, so what? She and Vincent could read it together. She had also made up her mind to go into Haifa to send Vincent a telegram.

CHAPTER THIRTEEN

Two days after I sent the telegram to Rachel I received one back from her. It was on the kitchen table when he I got home from school in the afternoon.

Vincent:
Am so sorry about your father. Got your letter and telegram. I love you. I miss you. I will be home soon to hold you. Sent letter to you.

Love, Rachel

When I read Rachel's telegram it was the first time I felt true joy in many, many days. It had been two weeks since my father died and since Rachel left for Israel. She was due home on October 16th. Just twelve more days.

Things were a little better at home. At night I still sometimes heard my mother weeping in her room. My sister did her best to keep from crying in front of my mother, as she knew it would set mom off.

My mother got a part time job doing alterations at Nunzio's tailor shop up the street from our house. It got her out of the house, which was good. I tried to concentrate on my schoolwork. Some of my courses were very interesting while others could put you to sleep in about two minutes. When I wasn't in school, I hung around with Mole and Eyeballs. We played a lot of basketball and handball.

The days seem to drag on. I still wasn't used to the fact that my father was gone and Rachel was away. Every morning when I woke up, it took me a few seconds to realize how much my world had changed. Then it would all hit me. Sometimes I felt like just falling back into bed. I just didn't want to face the world. I couldn't imagine what my mother felt like. She was a woman with remarkable courage. It must have been so hard for her to get up everyday and get on with her life. But she did it, and she inspired my sister and me.

On the night table next to my bed I kept a small calendar and had been marking off the days until Rachel came home. I had never done anything like that in my life. I knew she would be home on the sixteenth. Obviously, I couldn't just show up at Rachel's house when she got home. But I knew she would call me as soon as she had the chance on the day she got back to Brooklyn.

On October 14th Rachel took the bus to Haifa to send Vincent another telegram. Her plane was scheduled to leave Tel Aviv at eleven in the morning on the sixteenth. With the seven-hour time difference she would land in New York at about one in the afternoon. She wanted to let Vincent know she would come by his house around four o'clock that day. She'd spend a few hours with her family, then tell them she wanted to visit some friends. Of course, she'd head straight to Vincent's house.

She had never been so excited to leave a place as she was to leave the kibbutz. She missed her family and she missed Vincent terribly. The only thing she really learned by working on a kibbutz for twenty-four days is that she never wanted to work on a kibbutz again. Perhaps she wouldn't mind returning to Israel as a tourist one day, but that's all.

The letter and telegram from Vincent were in Rachel's suitcase, as was the bracelet. She didn't want to wear the bracelet into Haifa. She had packed most of her clothes already, just leaving out a couple of outfits for her last two days on the kibbutz. She was Jewish and Israel was the Jewish homeland, but she was a Brooklyn girl at heart. The nine-hour plane ride to New York would be a long one, but at the end of the journey she would see her family and she would see Vincent. She would be home again, in Brooklyn, where she belonged.

I got a telegram from Rachel on October 15th telling me what time she would be home the next day. I went to sleep early that night so the time would pass more quickly and I'd wake up on the sixteenth knowing I would see her.

I knew she had to spend time with her family once she got home, but I also knew that as soon as she could get away I would see her.

I woke up on the sixteenth feeling better than I had in a very long time. I knew in that a few hours I would be kissing Rachel and holding her. The hours passed very slowly. My mother and sister were excited for me and they were looking forward to seeing Rachel as well.

As the late afternoon approached I waited for the phone to ring, or for Rachel to show up at our door. Every time the phone rang I jumped, but it was never Rachel. The knock never came on the door. Afternoon turned into night and I still hadn't heard from her. Maybe she just couldn't get away from her family? Still, she would have found a way to call me, even if she had to sneak off to a payphone on the street.

By around eight o'clock that night every instinct in my body told me to walk over to Rachel's house, but I knew that wouldn't solve anything. Suppose I knocked on the door and her father answered? He would have no idea why I was there. What if I saw Rachel there? What was I going to do, take her in my arms and kiss her in front of her father? He didn't even know we were seeing each other. Her mother knew we were in love, but what good was that if her old man didn't know?

"I'm sure she just got caught up with her family," my mother said, trying to reassure me while we sat at the kitchen table.

"She would have found a way to call me or something," I said.

"Just be patient Vincent."

"I'm trying, ma, I'm really trying."

"Maybe you should just call her house."

"What am I going to say if her father answers? 'Hi, this is Vincent, your daughter and I are in love, but you don't know about it, can I please speak to her?' "

"I'm sure she'll call you Vincent. Listen, why don't you call, and if her father answers just hang up, and if her mother answers just tell her to have Rachel call you right away."

I did what my mother said. On the third ring a woman answered the phone whose voice I didn't recognize. It wasn't Mrs. Levy.

"Hello," she said.

I was silent for a moment. I didn't know what to do. If I told this woman it was Vincent calling for Rachel, the she'd probably yell to Rachel that Vincent was on the phone for her and that definitely wouldn't be good.

"Hello, who is this?" she said.

I heard voices in the background; the house was full of people.

"Yes," I said softly. "May I speak to Rachel?"

There was a moment of silence. Then the woman started screaming at me in Yiddish, I think, and hung up the phone.

My mother was standing next to me when I hung up the phone.

"Well, what happened?" she asked.

"I'm not really sure. Some strange woman answered the phone, and when I asked for Rachel, she started yelling at me in Yiddish and slammed the phone down."

"Vincent, I'm sure Rachel will contact you. I'm sure she just can't get away. Be patient."

I went to bed at around midnight and still hadn't heard from Rachel. I slept maybe three hours the whole night. I just kept tossing and turning. I had started out that day feeling like a little kid on Christmas Eve, and I ended the day feeling hurt, confused, frustrated and angry.

The following day I paced around the house all morning. Every time the phone rang I ran to answer it, but Rachel didn't call. At about one o'clock I sat down on our front stoop and stared out at the cars passing by on Coney Island Avenue. My mother came out the door and sat next to me.

"I'm sure you'll hear from her soon," she said.

"I can't believe she hasn't called me yet."

"I'm sure there has to be a good reason."

"I feel like I should just go over there."

"Do you think that's a good idea?"

"Maybe not, but I don't know what else to do."

"Vincent, you should eat something. You've hardly eaten anything in the last two days."

"I'm just not hungry, ma."

My mother stood up and rubbed my back.

"Don't worry, Vincent," she said, "you'll see her soon. If you get hungry come in the house and I'll make you something."

"Okay ma."

She went into the house and I sat on the stoop for another hour. I could hear the phone ring in the house a couple of times while I sat there, and I hoped my mother would call out to me that Rachel was on the phone, but she didn't.

I finally got up and went into the house. My mother was sitting in the den watching a soap opera on television. I sat down in my father's chair.

"Ma, I'm just going over there," I said.

"If that's what your heart tells you to do, then do it."

"I don't know what else to do."

"You can be a bit more patient."

"Ma, she's been away close to a month. How much more patient can I be? I don't know, I thought she was as anxious to see me as I was to see her."

"I'm sure she is."

"Then why hasn't she called, or come over here? Something's not right."

"Do you think maybe somehow her father found out about you two and forbid her to see you?"

"How could he find out unless Rachel told him?"

"Maybe she did."

"I don't think so. She'd tell me first. I know she would."

"Remember when you first told your father and me about you and Rachel?"

"Yeah."

"I said that you two would run into a lot of problems and I just didn't want you to get hurt?"

"Yeah, I know, ma."

"This is what I meant. I'm not saying that I told you so. But I hate to see you so hurt and miserable. You two have been seeing each other over a year, and still her father doesn't know. It's not right, Vincent. You love her and she loves you, and you should have been there at the airport when she got home. You should be with her right now. But you can't even go over there to see her because of this whole situation with her father."

"I know, ma, I know. When I see Rachel I'll tell her we just have to face up to her father. That's it. But I have to see her first."

"I wish I had an answer for you, Vincent. But I don't."

"I hate feeling so helpless, like there's nothing I can do."

"There's nothing you can do right now."

After another twenty minutes of pacing around the house and driving my mother crazy, I made up my mind to walk over to Rachel's house. It was about three in the afternoon. I had no intention of just knocking on the door. I just wanted to see what was going on over there. I was going to stand across the street from her house, and maybe there was a chance I would see her. Or maybe I would catch her coming out the door to come and see me.

I walked over and sat on a bench on the esplanade on the corner of Avenue U and Ocean Parkway opposite the Levy house. There were a lot of cars parked on the service road in front of her house, so I figured all her relatives were there to welcome her home. I sat for at least an hour and saw dozens of people coming and going from the Levy house, but I didn't see Rachel. A few times I almost worked up the courage to just go over there and knock on the door, but I knew that it wouldn't be a good idea.

I was about to leave when I saw the front door open one more time. Mr. Levy came out and stood on his front stoop staring out at Ocean Parkway. As he looked around he spotted me on the bench opposite his house. From across the parkway his eyes locked onto mine. My first instinct was to get up and walk away, but instead I just sat there. We looked at each other across Ocean Parkway for a moment, and then Mr. Levy began to walk toward me. I sat on the bench and waited for him. Maybe Rachel had told him about us and he was coming to tell me to stay away from his daughter. I felt I was ready for anything he had to say.

I wasn't.

As he approached the bench I stood up. He said nothing to me and sat down. He looked somber. I waited for him to say something. We just sat in silence for a moment.

"Mr. Levy," I said, "Rachel and I…."

"Vincent," he interrupted, "Rachel is gone."

"I know she was gone Mr. Levy, but she got home yesterday and I…."

"Vincent, you don't understand, she's gone."

I was confused.

"Gone where?" I asked. "What are you saying?"

Tears started to form in his eyes. A few rolled down his cheeks.

"My little girl is gone," he said softly.

At that moment I knew what he meant but I just couldn't accept it.

"Mr. Levy, What the hell are you telling me?"

He looked at me with tears in his eyes.

"She was killed in Israel, Vincent, two days ago"

What I felt at that moment I wouldn't wish on another human being. There are times in life when the shock, hurt and heartbreak are so enormous that no reaction is possible. I heard what Mr. Levy had told me but just couldn't comprehend it. It was as if my mind put up a wall and just refused to accept what I knew to be true in my heart.

"I knew about you and Rachel," Mr. Levy said through his tears. "I am not a blind man. I somehow knew in my heart. I had never seen my little girl so happy. She often told me she was going out with friends, but I knew where she was going. I knew she was seeing you. After the first few weeks it wasn't hard to figure out. What could I do? I knew her heart was full of love. I could see it in her. Her mother always knew. I had hoped that perhaps with her going to Israel you two might no longer see each other."

I stared at Mr. Levy in stunned disbelief and shock. My body was numb. There was a ringing in my ears and my eyes filled with tears.

"I knew, Vincent. I knew all along," he said. "This evening I had planned to come to your house to tell you about Rachel. You loved her and she loved you, and you had a right to know."

"What happened, Mr. Levy? I have to know," I said in a whisper.

He swallowed hard and stared straight ahead.

"Please, Mr. Levy, tell me" I pleaded, "I have to

know."

"There is much trouble in Israel. There is much bitterness and hate between the Palestinian Arabs and the Israelis. I fear it will always be like that. I fear it will only get worse......Rachel was on a bus. She was returning to the kibbutz from Haifa two days before she was to leave.....On a remote part of the road a group of Palestinians blocked the road with rocks and boulders. When the bus stopped they began throwing rocks at the bus. The driver got on the radio and contacted an Israeli army patrol unit. When they arrived they were fired upon by the Palestinians who had guns with them......There were many bullets fired until the Palestinians were chased away. Afterwards they checked the people on the bus. Ten of them were hit with stray bullets....Three were killed. Rachel was one of them."

Mr. Levy stared out across Ocean Parkway. Tears rolled down his face. I felt like I was going to explode from the inside. I wanted to scream, to cry, to run, all at the same time.

"Where did...." I mumbled. "Where did...why couldn't they....How...."

"The bullet went through her heart," he said. "She was killed instantly. They don't know if it was a Palestinian bullet or from an Israeli gun. Does it matter? Her body will arrive home tomorrow." He turned and looked at me. "Please come to the airport with us, Vincent. Rachel would have wanted you there to welcome her home."

At that moment I realized that one of the reasons

Rachel had taken the bus into the city of Haifa was to send me the telegram telling me when she was coming home. I could no longer control myself. The tears that had welled up in my eyes poured out of me. My body shook as I sobbed. I put my face in my hands. I felt Mr. Levy put his right arm around my shoulders, then his other arm encircled me. He hugged me tightly. I put my head in his chest and wept like I had never wept before. I felt his body begin to shake as well. I felt his tears as they fell and hit the back of my neck. We sat on the bench crying together for a long while.

I was with the Levy family at the airport the next day when Rachel came home from Israel. I learned that week that in the Jewish faith the body is interred the very next day, or as soon as possible after death. I stood with the Levy family at Rachel's funeral. My mother and sister were there as well. I also learned that Jewish people don't have wakes. Instead they mourn the death of a loved one by sitting *Shiva.* All the pictures and mirrors in the house are covered. No one sits on chairs or couches, instead they sit on boxes or stools. I sat Shiva with the Levys for a week after Rachel was buried.

On the day after Shiva ended, I was at my house lying on the couch in the den. It was about ten in the morning and I was alone. My mother was at work and my sister at school.

I was twenty-two years old and I felt like I just couldn't go on. Every day when I woke up I had this irrational hope that the events of the last month had been nothing more than a horrible nightmare. I hoped that I would hear my father getting ready to go to work, and later that day I would see Rachel. But then reality hit me and just sapped my strength and spirit. Of the four people I loved most in the world, I had lost two of them within a month.

My Grandma Teresa always used to say that God doesn't give you more than you can bear. Every morning when I awoke I questioned that. I just couldn't bear to face the day. I stopped going to school. I had no motivation to do anything except cry.

As I lie on the couch staring at the ceiling I heard a knock at the front door. When I opened it, I saw Mr. Levy standing on our front stoop.

"Hello Vincent," he said.

"Come in, Mr. Levy."

He came in and I led him to the den. I told him to sit in my father's chair. In his hand he held a brown envelope.

"I hope I am not intruding," he said.

"Of course not."

He took a deep breath.

"Rachel's possessions were returned to us when her body was returned home."

He held out the brown envelope to me.

"You should have these," he said.

I took the envelope from his hand. I opened it and inside was the letter and telegram I had sent Rachel, and wrapped in a piece of tissue was the diamond and emerald bracelet I had given her. I swallowed hard.

"Thank you," I said.

"I thought you should have those things."

"I appreciate it, Mr. Levy."

"I read the letter you wrote to Rachel."

I said nothing.

"I could not help myself," he said. "I had to read it."

Tears came to his eyes. He looked down at the floor then back at me.

"I realize only now how lucky Rachel was to have such a fine young man as you love her so much," he said softly. "And I know how much she loved you. I wish I had not been so rigid with her. I wish now she had felt comfortable enough to tell me about the love you two had for each other. It would have made her so happy. I will regret that for the rest of my life." He paused and took a handkerchief from the pocket of his vest to wipe the tears from his face. "Over this last week I have been so overcome with grief about my Rachel that I don't know if I ever expressed my sympathy to you and your family about the passing of your father. If I didn't, I apologize and please accept my condolences now."

"I understand, Mr. Levy, and thank you"

"You are a young man who has lost a great deal in a short time. I wish there was something I could do to help you."

"Mr. Levy, I don't think there's anything anyone can do to help either of us. I lost my father and the woman I love. You lost a child. Sometimes I don't know if it's even possible to go on."

"But you must go on."

"I don't know how."

"None of us know how, but we must."

"Sometimes I just don't think I can."

"Are you continuing in school?"

"No sir, I just can't bring myself to start going back to class."

"But you have to. You must. Do you think your father would have wanted you to stop?" Do you think my Rachel would have wanted you to stop?"

"No sir."

"Then why did you stop? I can understand taking some time off, but you must continue your education."

"I don't know. I just can't bring myself to do anything."

"Listen to me, Vincent. I understand your feelings. From the day I found out Rachel was gone until this very day I have had trouble even getting out of bed. But I know I must. I have a wife and two other children who count on me, just as I am sure your mother and sister count on you. I have to be strong for my family as you have to be strong for yours. We have both suffered great losses. But we must go on with our lives. You must move on with your life. Do it for your mother and your sister. Do it for your father. Do it for my Rachel. But most of all, do it for yourself, Vincent."

I knew Mr. Levy was right. He was a wise man.

As I walked him to the door that afternoon I thanked him again for bringing me the letter, the telegram and the bracelet.

"They belong to you," he said, "as my Rachel did."

I smiled for the first time in a very long time.

"I never thought I'd hear you say something like that," I said.

He smiled, too. "Vincent, please do not be a stranger. Please come by and see us when you can."

"I will, sir."

"Also, Vincent?"

"Yes sir?"

"I think I would like to maybe start watching baseball again. I haven't been to a game since the Dodgers left Brooklyn. Perhaps one evening you and I might attend a Mets game?"

"I would love to, Mr. Levy."

"Good then, we will go."

I shook Mr. Levy's hand and then we embraced each other. Both of us had tears in our eyes.

"Can you imagine what my Rachel is thinking in Heaven right now seeing us embracing as we are?" he said. "I know she is very happy. You made her happy Vincent. She loved you and that is the most precious gift in this world. I know that now."

"Rachel knew that, too."

As I watched Mr. Levy walk away from our house that day I felt a renewed strength within myself. Everything he told me was right. I knew that, and I was grateful for his wise words. Words a father would tell a son.

The following day I received even more inspiration to start living my life again.

CHAPTER FOURTEEN

The next day I took the bus to Borough Community College to speak with all my teachers. I told them why I had missed so many classes in the previous month, and asked if I could make up the work I had missed so I could continue on with my courses. All of them did everything they could to help me get back into the swing of things at school.

When I got home that afternoon I walked into the kitchen to get something to eat. My mother was sitting at the table. In her hands she held an envelope.

"Vincent, sit down," she said.

I sat opposite her.

"I came home from the tailor shop today to have some lunch and while I was here the mailman came," she continued. "He brought this, so I thought it best that I not go back to work."

She handed me the envelope. It had Israeli stamps on it and I immediately recognized Rachel's handwriting.

"Are you going to be okay?" mom asked.

"I'll be fine, ma."

"It's from Rachel, isn't it?"

"Yeah ma, I guess she mailed it a couple of weeks before she was supposed to leave. If you don't mind, ma, I'm going to go up to my room to read this."

"Sure Vincent, whatever you need to do."

I went upstairs to my bedroom and sat on my bed. I stared down at the envelope in my hands. Rachel was going to speak to me again.

October 4, 1963

My Dearest Vincent,

I am so sorry to hear about your father. I know how much you loved and respected him, and I know the pain and grief you feel must be unbearable. I wish I were there by your side right now. That's where I belong in this world, by your side. I wish I were there to hold you and comfort you. I will be home soon and I will never leave you again.

I was filled with joy when I got your letter. I was a little afraid of what it might say, but just seeing your name on the envelope made my heart leap. After I read what happened to your father I was greatly saddened and all I wanted in this world at that moment was to be with you. I knew in my heart all along that something must have happened to keep you from meeting me at the café on the day I left.

My time here on this kibbutz has been nothing but hard work everyday. All I do is pick pears all day in the hot sun. The second day I was here I got your bracelet caught on a branch while grabbing a pear and it was almost ripped off my wrist. After that, I took it off every morning before I went into the orchids and wrapped it in a piece of tissue paper. Then at night I put it back on. It is the symbol of our love and once I leave this place I'll never take it off again.

Being away from you has made me realize even more how much I love you. When I get home the first thing we are going to do is tell my father about us. You were right all along about that. Our love for each other is a beautiful thing and we shouldn't hide it from anybody, not even my father.

Every minute of every day that I've been here I think about you. It is such boring work picking pears, so I pass the time thinking of us. Thinking of the first time we met, meeting on the bench, going to the ball game, our special night on the beach at Coney Island. It is these thoughts of you that keep me going and make the time pass more quickly.

I bet by now you are the top student at Borough College. I know how much you were looking forward to going to school, and in my imagination I can see you sitting in class just like I sat in those same classrooms. Stick it out, Vincent, and graduate. That's what your father would have wanted for you. He would have wanted you to realize your dreams. It's what I want for you, too. I know that more than anything in this world you would want your father to be there on the day you graduate college. But he will be there in spirit, and he'll be proud of the fine man he raised. The man I love. And I'll be there, too, beaming with pride.

I'll be home in about two weeks to hold you and kiss you again. I can't wait to feel your arms around me again. To me, being in your arms is the best and safest place in the world. And always remember this, Vincent, you are the only man I will ever love.

I Love You - Your Rachel

OCTOBER, 1993

I graduated from college in 1965. I married my wife Sara later that year - two years after Rachel's death. I had met Sara in school about a year after Rachel died. To tell you the truth, although I was only in my early twenties at the time, I honestly didn't know if I could ever truly love again. But Sara was patient, kind and understanding. We started out as friends and became lovers. At first, I felt very guilty about my feelings for Sara. Something inside of me made me feel like I was betraying Rachel.

Shortly after I met Sara I had a dream about Rachel. To this day, it is the only time I have ever dreamed of her.

In the dream I am walking down the esplanade on Ocean Parkway. I look up and see Rachel sitting on the park bench by the bus stop near her house. I run to her and sit down. Suddenly I feel enormous guilt. I think that Rachel must know I have feelings for Sara. I look down at the ground ashamed of myself

"I'm so sorry," I say to Rachel.

"It's okay, Vincent," she says.

"I miss you so much. I think of you everyday."

"Vincent, look at me," she says.

I look up into her face. She is as beautiful as the first day I saw her.

"Vincent, it's okay. I love you. I want you to be happy."

"I'm sorry, Rachel," I say, and stare down at the ground again. Then I hear her voice.

"Vincent, listen to me," she says softly. "You always told me that you put the people you love ahead of yourself, and you always protect them. I love you Vincent and I want you to be happy. It's okay to love again."

I look up, but Rachel is no longer on the bench next to me. I hear a bus coming up Avenue W. It stops on the corner and I see Rachel boarding the bus. I yell out to her but she doesn't turn around. She boards the bus. As the bus begins to move, she walks to the middle of the bus and sits down. I see her through the window. I can see my father sitting next to her.

Both of them smile as the bus disappears down Avenue W.

On the morning I woke up from the dream I had tears in my eyes. I knew I would forever have Rachel and my father in my heart, but I knew too that I had to move on with my life. On that morning I also realized, for the first time, how truly lucky I was to have known and loved them in the time we had together. I am not a very religious person, but sometimes I get this feeling that somehow Rachel and my father got together in Heaven and decided to come to me in a dream to show me the way.

I have never gone into great detail with my wife about my time with Rachel. She knows of our romance and how Rachel died. That's about it. How can I ever tell my wife, who I do love dearly, that there is a part of me that will never belong to her - a part of me that will always belong to Rachel Levy?

My daughter was born in September of 1966 and six years later Sara gave birth to our twin boys, Angelo and Franco.

I got my first job as a photographer with the *New York Daily News* in early 1966. Since then I have worked for a short time for both the *New York Times* and the *New York Post*. I finally landed at *Time Magazine* and have spent the majority of my career with them.

I have traveled all over the world taking photos and writing about what I've seen. I have spent much time in the Middle East covering the various conflicts and wars in that region of the world. Mr. Levy was right all those years ago when he told me that he feared things would only get worse.

The first time I was in Israel I visited the kibbutz near Haifa and found the spot on the road to Haifa where Rachel lost her life. It's still dangerous territory. It always will be.

It has been thirty years since I lost Rachel, but I think of her always. I still live in Brooklyn and often pass the places Rachel and I went to during our year together.

Mr. Levy passed away from throat cancer in 1968. I think he really died of a broken heart. He was never the same man after his Rachel died. He and I went to a number of New York Mets games together in the years before he passed away. We always had a good time, and he always made me tell him the story of the game I took Rachel to in 1962.

Mrs. Levy still lives in the big house on Ocean Parkway. I visit her every once and a while and we have a cup of coffee together. Seeing her reminds me of Rachel because they look so much alike. I often wonder how Mrs. Levy has the strength to go on. She lost her family in the Holocaust, she lost her oldest child, and then her husband. She is a woman of remarkable strength and courage and I admire her greatly. How life could be so cruel to such a wonderful woman is beyond my powers to explain or even comprehend.

In 1969 *Time Magazine* assigned me to cover the Vietnam Peace talks in Paris. I took Mrs. Levy with me.

"Why do you want me to go to Paris with you?" she asked as we sat at her kitchen table drinking coffee a few weeks before I left for France.

"I want to fulfill one of Rachel's dreams," I said.

"I don't understand."

"Mrs. Levy, Rachel told me one time about the couple in France that helped you after you escaped from the camp."

"Rachel told you my story?" she asked, somewhat shocked.

"No, she didn't tell me the whole story. She only told me of the Gagnons, the family that sheltered you from the Germans and nursed you back to health, and how it was a dream of yours to visit Mrs. Gagnon someday."

"It always has been a dream of mine."

"I know, but it was Rachel's dream, too. She told me that it was her dream to someday send you to France to visit. I know Mrs. Gagnon is still alive, but she's getting old and it's time for you to see her. Her farm is only a couple of hours from Paris"

"You don't have to do this, Vincent."

"I want to do it, Mrs. Levy. For you and Rachel."

The day after we arrived in Paris I drove Mrs. Levy to the Gagnon farm. It was about two hours north of the city. I took along a French colleague of mine who spoke English so Mrs. Levy and Mrs. Gagnon could converse. Mrs. Gagnon greeted Mrs. Levy like a long lost daughter. Mrs. Gagnon knew of the tragedies that had befallen Mrs. Levy from the letters they had exchanged over the years.

I had to stay in Paris but had arranged for Mrs. Levy to stay with Mrs. Gagnon a few days before she returned to the States. On the day Mrs. Levy had to leave France, I picked her up at the farm to drive her to the airport. Mrs. Gagnon greeted me at the door when I arrived. She gave me a big hug. Mrs. Levy stood behind her.

"Mr. Vincent," Mrs. Gagnon said in broken English. "I want to thank you for bringing Anna here. You have made the dreams of two old women come true. I cannot thank you enough."

Mrs. Levy smiled. "She's been practicing saying that in English all day."

Mrs. Gagnon hugged me again. Then Mrs. Levy hugged me.

When we arrived at the airport I walked Mrs. Levy

to her gate. Before she boarded the plane she turned to me.

"Vincent, I don't know what to say or how to thank you. There are no words"

"Mrs. Levy it was a dream of yours and Rachel's for you to come here. So it became my dream. You have helped me to realize one of my dreams. So I should be thanking you."

She hugged me tightly before she got on the plane. "Come and visit me when you get back to Brooklyn," she said. And she smiled. To see her smile like that was all the thanks I would ever need. She looked just like Rachel when she smiled.

My mom sold the house on Coney Island Avenue in 1980 and moved to a condo in Sunrise, Florida. She's in her seventies now and spends most of her time worrying about her children and her grandchildren. Some things never change. My sister Marie married a New York City firefighter and lives in Staten Island. They have three sons.

My best friend Mole never made it to the Yankees. In his fourth year in the minor leagues the Yankees promoted him to their highest farm team. He was one step away from being called up to the big leagues. Then, in a meaningless game at the end of that summer, Mole tore up the ligaments in his right knee sliding into second base. He had surgery to repair the injury but was never the same after that.

As a catcher, the constant squatting caused the knee to fill with water after every game. The Yankees gave up on him. He bounced around in the minor leagues for three more years before deciding to call it a career. He came home to Brooklyn and worked in his father's butcher shop for a while. Then one day, at age twenty-eight, he decided to join the Marines.

"Are you out of your mind?" I said to him when he told me.

"I gotta get outta Brooklyn," he said.

"Jesus Mole, you joined the Army reserve so you wouldn't get drafted and you could play ball. You did your military duty. And now you join the Marines? You wanna get outta Brooklyn? Then take the D train to the Bronx or something. What the hell did you join the Marines for? They're probably gonna send you to Vietnam."

"Yeah, I know."

"Are you crazy?"

"Don't worry, Bricks, I'll be fine. You know me. Nothin's gonna happen to the Mole."

Eyeballs Casola and I were pallbearers at Mole's funeral when they shipped his body home from Vietnam.

I had spent some time in Vietnam as a war correspondent in 1968. When I was there I had the chance to see Mole. We met in a bar in Saigon. He was in a combat unit and they had come back to Saigon for a week of R & R. I saw him only two days before his unit went back into combat. He was a corporal by then. He never changed. He was always the same cocky, confident guy I grew up with. He told me not to worry about him. "Hey Bricks," he said, "you know nothing is gonna happen to me. Don't worry about nothin'. I'll be fine."

I left Vietnam the next day and Mole stepped on a landmine three days later. Eyeballs told me about it. He had taken over his family's deli after his father died, and I went in there to see him a few days after I got back from Vietnam. I found him crying behind the counter. Mole's kid sister had just been in to tell Eyeballs that our friend was dead.

My little girl has grown up and become quite a beautiful woman. She works as a photographer for the *New York Daily News* and is a huge baseball fan. My twin boys are in college.

Whenever I see my daughter we often talk about the day in 1969 when I took her to see the Mets win their first World Championship at Shea Stadium. She was only three at the time and has some vague memories of that day. I remember it in great detail.

It was October 16th, 1969. October 16th, 1963 was the day Rachel was supposed to have arrived home from Israel. To me, it somehow seemed fitting that the "Miracle Mets" became champions on that same day six years later.

When the last out of the game was made the stadium absolutely erupted. For two hours afterwards people celebrated on the field and in the stands. Finally, the place started to empty out but I still sat in my seat looking out over the field with my little girl on my lap.

"The Mets won, right daddy?" she said to me.

"Yeah baby, the Mets are World Champions."

"That's good."

"Ready to go home now, baby?"

"Yes, daddy, let's go."

I stood up, holding her in my arms, and started to walk up the steps to the exit.

"No daddy," she said, "I want to walk."

I put her down and took her right hand.

She looked at up me. "Ready daddy?"

"Yes I am," I said. "Let's go home, Rachel."

****

ABOUT THE AUTHOR

Marino Amoruso is an award-winning writer, director, producer and author. He has written, directed and edited over 50 films for networks such as *PBS, The History Channel, Fox Sports Network, ESPN, The Arts and Entertainment Network, Madison Square Garden Network, Metro Sports, Lifetime, USA Network, Documentary Channel* and many others. He has been nominated for four Emmy Awards, won the prestigious Western Heritage Award, and has won awards at the New York Film Festival. He has also written three other books - *Gil Hodges: The Quiet Man, Our Contributions: The Italians in America* and *The Italians: A Musical History. Across 7th Street* is his first novel. His 2011 docudrama *Jackie Robinson: My Story,* won the Best Picture Award at the Long Island International Film Expo and the Garden State Film Festival.. He has three children, two stepchildren, two dogs and lives with his wife Myra in Oakdale, New York. For more information, visit **www.NSEfilms.com.**

13539153R00140

Made in the USA
Charleston, SC
16 July 2012